SPOTTING A CASE OF MURDER

PENELOPE BANKS MURDER MYSTERIES
BOOK 9

COLETTE CLARK

DESCRIPTION

Romance is in the air…and so is murder!

New York 1926
Penelope "Pen" Banks's neighbor, Mrs. Dorothy Abernathy, has vanished. At first, all indications suggest the lonely widow may have done herself in, despite the lack of a body.

But why didn't she provide for her beloved Dalmatians, Dot & Dash?

That little wrinkle is enough for Penelope to suspect something more sinister is afoot. With the help of Mrs. Abernathy's cheerful dog minder, Alice Winterfort, they dig deeper.

Soon enough, Pen learns her neighbor wasn't quite so lonely after all, and in fact had a rather *robust* romantic life. With no less than four possible suitors on her plate, there are numerous suspects to choose from.

So, which of her not-so-secret admirers may have killed her?

Spotting a Case of Murder **is the ninth book in the Penelope Banks Mystery series set in 1920s New York. A fun romp of a Valentine's Day historical mystery.**

CHAPTER ONE

"It's enough to make one positively mad, Penelope, mad to the point of—"

"Murder?" Penelope "Pen" Banks asked her older Cousin Cordelia, one eyebrow provocatively arched as she enjoyed an afternoon gin cocktail in the library that overlooked Central Park. Her cousin took the armchair across from her at the window.

"Don't say such sinful things, dear, it's the Sabbath." Cousin Cordelia arched a brow of her own in judgment. "Which you would know if you didn't always somehow manage to oversleep when it comes time to leave for church."

"I just find Reverend Ford a bit too fire and brimstone for my liking. Why not preach all the positive messages from the Bible? It would make the service so much more enjoyable."

"Church is no place for enjoyment," Cousin Cordelia said with a firm set to her mouth.

"It's February, exactly one week from Valentine's Day. I

shudder to think what his sermon will be next Sunday. Samson and Delilah? Adam and Eve? Probably something dreadful like the virtues of purity, modesty, or humility in women," Pen turned her mouth down in thought. "Now that I think of it, there are quite a few naughty women in the Bible."

"Speaking of naughty women," Cousin Cordelia said, giving Pen a pointed look. "If you had gone to church with me, you would have heard those dogs across the hall barking, both leaving *and* returning. And to think I always considered Dorothy Abernathy one of the more sensible residents of the building, though I must confess that I rarely saw her. Still, to let her pets behave such that the neighbors can hear them carrying on so is just plain rude."

"That is odd. I almost never hear them, even when that sweet girl, Alice comes by to take them outside for their walk."

"They are no doubt still at it as we speak. This is why I prefer cats. You'll never find Lady Dinah or even that little terror of yours upsetting the neighbors," Cousin Cordelia said in reference to her white Persian cat and her marmalade son, who could no longer be called a kitten as he was now bigger than his mama.

"Little Monster wreaks his own form of havoc on me. And Lady Di is content to allow you to spoil her," Pen said before taking another sip. "Why didn't you just knock on Mrs. Abernathy's door and suggest she do something about it? They've probably been kept inside for so long because of the snow this past week. Granted, that beautiful layer of white from Thursday's storm is now a brown slush."

"Don't be silly, Pen. What would she think of me intruding like that?"

Pen set her glass down and gave her older cousin a

teasing smile. "Do you want *me* to go over and tell her how disruptive it is? You probably aren't the only one on this floor who is disturbed by them."

"Penelope, no!" Cousin Cordelia said in horror. She lowered her gaze and pursed her lips. "Though, perhaps a simple welfare check to make sure she hasn't gone completely deaf might be appreciated."

"I'll be the epitome of tact," Pen said, rising to leave.

Cousin Cordelia looked doubtful. Speaking of naughty women, meddlesome was the oft-used descriptor when it came to Penelope. That and mischievous, which explained her cousin's skepticism about how tactful she would actually be.

Still, Penelope was curious, perhaps even a bit worried. Mrs. Abernathy's dogs, Dot and Dash, were typically well-behaved from what she had seen. Also, the doors to the apartments at the Alstonian were fairly thick. For them to bark loudly enough for someone in the hallway to hear, there must have been something wrong.

Pen smoothed down her dark bobbed hair and headed to her front door. She opened it and looked across at the door to apartment 11B. She didn't hear anything, so she stepped into the hallway. As soon as she did, the barking started, interspersed by several pitiful whines.

Yes, something was definitely amiss in Apartment 11B.

She quickly closed the distance to the door and knocked. That quieted the dogs for only a second before they began again, more urgently. She could hear them scratching at the door, which definitely wasn't a good sign.

"Mrs. Abernathy?" Pen called loudly. She knocked much harder and repeated herself even louder. "Mrs. Abernathy? Are you there?"

There was no answer and Pen frowned as she stared at

the door. Her eyes fell to the lock and she flirted with the idea of picking it. It would have been good practice. She reminded herself that it was the Alstonian not the apartment of some criminal suspect. Even if the circumstances seemed dire, there were more appropriate avenues before resorting to breaking and entering.

"Don't worry," Pen said to the dogs. "I'm going to get someone."

She rushed to the elevator. Only once she was on it, did she remember how slowly it progressed. While it was quite beautiful—a gold and white Art Nouveau style, fashioned after Otto Wagner's in Austria—it was rather tedious when one was in a hurry. Pen tapped her foot with impatience as the elevator eased down to the lobby. She was relieved to see that there was nothing requiring the doorman's attention at the moment. He stood up straighter behind his desk when he saw her exit.

"Good afternoon, Miss Banks."

"Hello, Eugene, I'm afraid I may need some assistance up on the eleventh floor. Have you seen Mrs. Abernathy, my neighbor, lately?"

"Well, I saw her going out Friday afternoon, same time as usual the past several weeks. You know they have me working afternoons, so I usually see her returning from wherever she's gone to during the day, then she often goes right back out again in the evening, dressed for dinner out."

He saw a woman approaching the front door and interrupted himself to rush and open it for her. She knew the woman lived on the fourth floor, having taken the elevator with her once. Pen had been in the building a little over a year and thus recognized almost everyone. Her mind worked almost like a camera, capturing everything like a photograph for her memory.

"Good afternoon, Mrs. Duncan," Eugene said, tipping his hat.

He returned to the desk. "Where was I?"

"You were telling me about the last time you'd seen Mrs. Abernathy?"

"Ah yes, well it was Friday afternoon, around three, I think it was. She had on that white fur coat of hers, which I think was a mistake since all that snow we got on Wednesday and Thursday had already turned ugly. It's the cars. Dirty tires, dirty smoke. You never saw that with horses, though I suppose the streets would have been nothing but mud then. But she didn't seem to mind, even told me how much she'd miss the snow. Spring will be here soon enough, I suppose. Still, a good thing she took a taxi, what with her nice shoes and expensive jewelry on. I suppose she had someplace important to be."

Now Pen was glad for his loquaciousness. He had told her quite a bit that helped create a picture of where her neighbor might have been going, obviously something more than a simple errand or casual visit if she was wearing noticeably expensive jewelry. The fur was understandable, considering how frigid the air was.

"And you didn't see her come back?"

"No. Like I said, Monday through Thursday she was often in, then back out again, happy as a clam. Fridays she went out in the afternoons and didn't come back on my watch. You know, for being in her late fifties, she's a spry one that Mrs. Abernathy. I don't know what she gets up to, but it's certainly more fun than opening doors and accepting deliveries." He chuckled.

Pen didn't think Mrs. Abernathy would be quite so amused if she knew her age was being bandied about in such a manner. Then again, some women relished reaching a certain period in their lives, one in which they were less concerned about impressing others. Pen had reached that age early on, having experienced a fall from grace when her father cut her off several years ago.

"So, as far as you know she could still be gone?" Pen asked.

He frowned. "Well, she only had her small valise with her as usual. Rodney, who works mornings could tell you if she returned yesterday morning." He cleared his throat uncomfortably as though cognizant as to what that hinted at.

"I see," Pen said, pretending to ignore his faux pas. "It's just that her two dogs, Dot and Dash, have been barking up a storm this morning. I'm a bit worried is all. I know she has a housemaid and a cook, but no one is answering."

"Gosh, I certainly hope nothing's happened. She's one of the nicer residents. Gave us a mighty nice bonus this year, much more than usual." He cleared his throat again. "Though, we all very much appreciated the bonus you gave us Miss Banks. It was very generous as well."

Penelope should have been somewhat appalled at his frank chatter, but for the moment it was quite useful. She had given what she'd thought was a generous amount, but it seemed Mrs. Abernathy had gone above and beyond even that, more than usual according to Eugene. Still, Pen reminded herself to be more circumspect around him in the future.

"You're welcome, Eugene. It's a very helpful service you offer. And I'd truly hate to think of Mrs. Abernathy being in her apartment all alone, perhaps injured or worse. Her staff doesn't seem to be in at the moment." Pen's bright blue eyes were wide with the hint.

"Yes, that would be bad."

"With the dogs barking incessantly."

"That must be quite irritating."

Pineapples! Penelope cursed to herself. For all his attention to detail and lack of tact, Eugene was being rather slow to catch on.

"Yes, well, I'm more worried than anything. Perhaps she came back when one of the other doormen was on duty and she suffered an accident? She could be lying there right now, injured, and Dot and Dash are the only ones who can tell us something is wrong. Perhaps that explains the barking?"

His eyes lit up with understanding. "You want I should check on her?"

"You *do* have a master key."

"Yes, well..." He seemed uncertain. "I don't know about entering a resident's apartment without permission."

"Of course," she said, nibbling her bottom lip in thought. She didn't blame him for being cautious in that regard. It was the kind of thing that could get a doorman fired. "You know, I have a detective friend—"

"Detective Prescott! Yes, I've met him, the one with the scar."

"Yes, well perhaps he could come and be of assistance."

"That would definitely make me feel better about the whole thing."

"I'll do that," she said briskly. "Can I use the phone at your desk rather than go all the way back up to my apartment?"

"Of course, anything for Mrs. Abernathy."

Pen picked up the phone and connected with him using the number that was by now etched in her memory.

Detective Richard Prescott was more than just a friend at this point. Pen was hoping he would be cognizant of that when she made a request for him to come over just to check on two barking dogs.

CHAPTER TWO

"We really appreciate you coming, Detective Prescott," Penelope said, making sure to use his professional address just to maintain some semblance of authority as he accompanied Eugene and her up to the eleventh floor of the Alstonian.

"It's all a part of my duties, Miss Banks," Richard said, giving her a wry smile.

Eugene had called upon one of the weekend maintenance men to cover the front desk while he accompanied them, since he had the master key to get into Mrs. Abernathy's apartment.

Behind Eugene's back, she shot him an appreciative smile, as usual admiring how handsome he was, with a strong jaw and dark eyes framed by full lashes. Many women would have noted the scarring rising out of his collar and creeping up to just below his right jaw and ear and offered another descriptor. Even without knowing he had received it during the Great War, Penelope thought it made him devilishly dashing.

"Yeah, I was really hesitant to do this on my own,"

Eugene said. "I mean, I appreciate Miss Banks's concern and all, but if this turns out to be nothing and we end up walking in on Mrs. Abernathy in nothing but her—"

"As I said, it's all a part of my duties."

The elevator, as beautiful as it was, eased along at a glacial pace. Pen tried to keep from tapping her toe as floor after floor passed by. When they reached the eleventh floor, they could hear Mrs. Abernathy's dogs barking before Eugene could finish opening the gates to the elevator.

"They are indeed barking," Eugene said, sounding relieved that this hadn't been for naught.

"Indeed they are," Richard confirmed.

As they approached, the barking got more frantic, and was once again interspersed with whining and scratching at the door.

"Do you see what I mean?" Penelope said.

Richard rapped on the door, loudly enough for anyone inside to hear. Still, the only answer was continued barking.

Across the hall, the door to Penelope's apartment opened. Cousin Cordelia stuck her head out. The avid curiosity written on her face explained why Chives, their butler, hadn't been the one to open the door for her. They were still without a maid of their own. That was probably for the best, after a year fraught with ill luck in that department.

"Mrs. Davies," Richard said diplomatically. "I certainly hope we weren't disturbing you."

Cousin Cordelia eased out of the apartment. "Oh no, I just thought I could perhaps be of service."

Penelope arched an eyebrow in skepticism. She knew full well that her cousin was being a busybody, hoping to sneak a look into the apartment of their neighbor.

"I think we'll be fine, Cousin. After all, I'd hate for you

to suffer some unfortunate sight, should the worst have occurred to poor Mrs. Abernathy."

Cousin Cordelia's bottom lip stuck out with petulance. Before she could object, Richard agreed with Pen.

"Miss Banks is right, Mrs. Davies. I think perhaps it's best you stay out here until we know what has happened."

"I suppose," she said begrudgingly, but she remained in the hallway.

The dogs were showing their impatience at the interlude and everyone turned their attention back to the door.

"You think it's a good idea to open it?" Eugene said, wanting official permission directly from Detective Prescott.

"At this point, I need you to open the door, if only to check on the welfare of the animals, Mr...?"

"You can just call me Eugene." He took a breath and pulled out the key to unlock it. He opened it a crack and called out, "Mrs. Abernathy?"

The dogs had gone quieter, now just eagerly sniffing at the crack and whining. Otherwise, all was quiet. Even the lights were out. Eugene opened the door wider, and he was instantly attacked by a rush of white with black spots. Both dogs leaped up, their front paws on his pants.

"Allow me to enter first," Richard said, placing a staying hand on his shoulder. He took advantage of the fact that the dogs were preoccupied with Eugene to enter the apartment unmolested. Penelope quickly followed, entering the foyer with black and white checkerboard tiles that matched the coloring of the dogs.

There was enough light seeping through the heavy curtains overlooking Central Park to guide him. He walked over and, with one sweep, he pushed them aside to allow the sun, now in the western half of the sky, to drench the apartment in light.

Other than the dogs, who Eugene was still trying to settle, everything seemed eerily still. Penelope had never been in Mrs. Abernathy's apartment and took a moment to look around mostly out of curiosity.

Like the residence Penelope had inherited from Agnes Sterling—along with several million dollars—she knew the living room, and library both overlooked Central Park. She knew it was a smaller apartment, with only two bedrooms. The master bedroom most likely overlooked the park, while the second bedroom and dining room would probably face the inner courtyard.

Pen took a moment to study the living room. The overall theme seemed to be flowers. There were multiple vases of lush red roses with sprigs of baby's breath, that couldn't have been more than a couple of days old. Every wall was either painted in a soft blush or decorated with floral wallpaper. On most of them hung paintings that could only be described as cloyingly idyllic: cozy cottages tucked in colorfully verdant gardens of buttercups, petunias, hydrangeas, and other flowers.

There was a small card on the table next to one of the vases of flowers:

My love,

Please forgive me. I'm sure you know what these flowers mean. I shall be waiting at our usual place tomorrow.

Yours

There was no name. In fact, the note told her almost

nothing. Had he been the one Mrs. Abernathy had been meeting on Fridays? It suggested the roses had been sent on Thursday, if so.

Pen continued to look around. On almost every free surface sat small, romantic figurines of pink-cheeked women holding flowers, or young lovers set amid floral scenes. Considering how many there were, Mrs. Abernathy was obviously a collector.

"Oh, a Lachapelle!" Cousin Cordelia, who had obviously decided it was safe to enter, exclaimed with glee. She walked over to pick one up. "Harold bought me one of these early on in our marriage. My, but they are certainly dear. It broke and I fretted over him ever buying me another. How does she have so many?"

"I'm thinking maybe these dogs are whining for a reason," Eugene said in a pleading voice.

"Yes, let's check to make sure they have food and water," Penelope replied.

She led Eugene into the kitchen, which seemed the most likely place to find the dogs' dish bowls. Dot and Dash rushed ahead of them. It was an interior room with no windows so she couldn't see much at first. She did, however, note the unfortunate smell upon entering.

That wasn't a good sign.

Pen turned on the lights and saw what was causing the smell. It almost looked as though the dogs had been sick, poor things.

"Jeez, when were these dogs last taken for a walk?"

"You don't know?" Pen asked.

"The girl who usually takes them out has her own key and uses the service elevator at the side of the building. Not many residents are too keen on sharing the resident elevator with two large dogs."

"Of course," Pen said. She'd only seen Alice Winterfort in the hallways with nothing more than a pleasant hello after their first introduction. Granted, the young woman was usually trying to control two dogs eager to get outside.

Pen walked around the island to find the dogs' dishes and bowls. There was nothing in the food dishes other than filthy streaks from them licking the bowl. Next to them sat two silver bowls with only droplets of water remaining.

"Oh you poor things," Penelope lamented. She quickly picked up both bowls and rushed to the sink to fill them. Pen hadn't even set them down before both dogs were at their respective bowls eagerly lapping away. "How long have you two gone without anything to eat or drink?"

Either Alice was neglecting her duties, or something else was going on. Pen checked all the cupboards, the larder, and the ice box and found everything almost empty. Even the sugar and flour canisters were empty.

"She has no food at all, not even for her dogs!" Pen exclaimed. She glanced down at Dot and Dash with a frown. "I suppose there may be a bit of ground chuck from my kitchen. If not, I'll send for some. I suspect these two haven't eaten in a while. When did you last see her cook or maid, Eugene?"

"They usually come in by the service entry as well, so I really don't see them."

"Of course. Has Mrs. Abernathy said anything about going away, perhaps on an extended trip?"

"No."

"Is that something she'd normally tell you about?"

"Usually it's pretty obvious. Most residents like to chat about some long holiday or weekend trip they're looking forward to. Come to think of it, I've worked here two years and I don't think I've ever seen Mrs. Abernathy take any trips."

Richard came to join them in the kitchen. "I can't find any sign of her in the apartment, or any staff for that matter. I knocked on the door to the staff quarters with no answer."

"Yes, and it seems she left both the dogs and herself without any food and water. Eugene says she hadn't mentioned anything about going away on an extended holiday or anything. I'm officially worried."

"There is one thing I'd like to show you that may perhaps explain—"

"Hello? Who's in here?" He was interrupted by a young woman's voice reaching them from the front door. The three of them walked back into the living room where Cousin Cordelia was still admiring the figurines and paintings. A pretty young woman was entering from the foyer. She stared back at them, eyes wide with surprise and suspicion.

"What exactly is going on here?"

"We were hoping you could tell us, Alice," Penelope responded.

CHAPTER THREE

Alice Winterfort, who saw to Mrs. Abernathy's dogs, was a pretty young thing, only about twenty years old. She had large, sparkling brown eyes and a button nose. Her cheeks sported a smattering of freckles she didn't bother hiding with powder. Her dark hair was cut down to her neck and curled at the ends. Her mouth naturally settled into a smile that only became brighter when she was truly happy, which was often. Then again, Pen only saw her when she was on her way to or from taking care of the dogs, who she seemed to adore as much as they did her.

That day, she was in a festive red coat to fight the winter chill and a matching red, knit tam with a jaunty puff on top.

"What's going on?" Alice demanded, sounding slightly panicked at seeing so many people in the apartment.

"Alice, this is Detective Prescott, a friend of mine. Richard, this is Alice Winterfort. She sees to Dot and Dash. Alice, the dogs seem to have been left alone for at least a few days, and we can't find any sign of Mrs. Abernathy or her staff. The last Eugene saw of her was Friday afternoon. Perhaps you can explain what is going on?"

Before Alice could answer, Dot and Dash came rushing to her, tails wagging gloriously, their thirst apparently sated.

"Hiya, girls!" Alice sang, falling to her knees to nuzzle and pet them.

"Seeing as how Mrs. Abernathy's girl is here, I should probably get back to the desk," Eugene hinted.

"Of course," Richard said. "Thank you for letting us in. I'll be down if I have any more questions."

Pen turned her attention back to Alice, still engaged with the dogs, once Eugene left. "I became worried when I heard those two barking nonstop and asked Eugene to open the door for us. We found their food and water dishes completely empty, and I don't think they've been taken out recently, based on the mess I've seen in the kitchen."

"That couldn't be!" Alice seemed perfectly aghast. She looked down at the poor dogs with profound apology. "Now I wish I'd come by to drop off my key earlier. Mrs. Abernathy said I could do it any time this weekend. You poor girls must have been in such a state!"

"Drop off your key? So you're no longer employed by her?" Pen asked.

"No," Alice said, her focus still on the dogs. "Mrs. Abernathy said she no longer needed my service, so I was returning to give her back the key. I just returned from visiting my family in Brooklyn."

"Was Mrs. Abernathy unhappy with your services?" Pen couldn't believe such a thing considering how much Dot and Dash obviously loved her.

"Oh no, in fact, she gave me quite a lovely parting sum. Far more than she should have."

"Did she tell you what her plans were?"

Alice shook her head, now looking worried. "No, but she never would have been so neglectful of her girls. Listen, if it's true they haven't been out since Friday, I should really take them outside."

"Of course. And I'll try and scrounge up something for them to eat. The kitchen is completely empty of food."

"Oh no!" Alice looked as though she was going to cry as she buried her face into one of the dogs' side. "Oh, you poor things. Yes, please do. They probably haven't eaten for days!"

"When did *you* last see to the dogs?" Pen asked, following Alice to a small closet where the leashes were.

"Thursday morning. I got a good walk in before the worst of the snow hit. Mrs. Abernathy told me I didn't have to come that afternoon or Friday, due to the heavy storm. She was going to have Sally, the maid, take them out for a bit. But if they haven't had anything since then... Oh, you poor things!" Alice cried hugging one of the dogs.

"Let me go see about some food for them."

Penelope rushed out of the apartment, closely followed by Cousin Cordelia.

"It's an attractively decorated apartment, don't you think? Such a lovely shade of pink on the walls, and all those flowers! We should hire a service to deliver roses regularly. Not to speak ill of the dead, but Agnes's choice of decor was rather modern for my tastes. Perhaps a bit of chintz on the walls or curtains wouldn't hurt?"

"You are perfectly welcome to put as much chintz as you'd like in your bedroom, dear Cousin," Pen said as tactfully as she could. She would have rather burned the apartment to the ground than allow it anywhere else. Penelope happened to like the way Agnes had decorated the apartment and saw no reason to change it when Cousin Cordelia and she moved in.

They entered the kitchen and found Arabella, her cook.

"The poor dogs across the hall haven't had anything to eat, possibly in days. You wouldn't have a little something to give them, would you?"

"The two lovely Dalmatians? Oh, the poor dears! Not to worry, Arabella always has her larders full, doesn't she?"

She rifled through the ice box and found some ground chuck to offer, still wrapped in paper. Pen thanked her and rushed back to the apartment. Cousin Cordelia, her curiosity presumably satisfied, decided to stay.

Back in Mrs. Abernathy's apartment, Pen divided the meat between both bowls. Dot and Dash went after it as ravenously as they had the water.

While they ate, Pen showed Alice the card, presumably sent with the flowers. "Do you know who this person is?"

Alice shook her head. "I have no idea. She never confided that sort of thing in me."

Richard approached them. "Can I show you two something in the bedroom? I think it might explain things."

"Mrs. Abernathy's bedroom?" Alice asked, an uncertain look on her face.

"I had to search everywhere to make sure she wasn't here."

They followed Richard into the bedroom, passing by the library and dining room. The large master bedroom was another vision in soft pink, with a lot of satin and gauzy fabric. Richard led them into her large closet. On the floor, there were several trunks, some looking as though they had just been purchased. Otherwise, the shelves and racks were empty.

"It looks like she was moving," Alice said.

"Or going on a very long trip. The rest of the apartment doesn't seem to show any evidence of moving out," Pen said.

Alice shrugged. "But why would she have let me go?

Especially if she wasn't going to feed the dogs. Where is their food? Sally, the maid isn't particularly fond of taking Dot and Dash out. Mrs. Abernathy wouldn't have left her to see to them long-term. All she ever does is walk them across the street to do their business and come back in. And it couldn't have been a matter of money. She pays me two dollars a day, and the amount she gave to me when she let me go was quite a bit more than that, a *lot* more." Alice's eyes were wide with wonder, as though confirming the generous amount.

"Perhaps Mrs. Abernathy planned on taking them with her wherever she was going. That might have explained the lack of dog food. Though, where has she been since Friday? It's now Sunday."

"And her staff has left as well. I checked their quarters and all traces of them are gone." Richard pointed out.

"The biggest question is where *is* Mrs. Abernathy?" Pen stared down at the trunks. "Perhaps we should open them to look inside, if only to help us learn more?"

"That's not a bad idea," Richard said, already pushing one of the newer ones out into the bedroom where there was more room and lighting.

"I should really take Dot and Dash outside for their walk. They've probably been going mad, cooped up in here the past few days."

"Of course, we'll try and do some more sleuthing while you're gone," Pen said.

Alice, still in her coat and hat, rushed back out. Pen heard the dogs barking in a way that sounded decidedly merrier than what she had first heard through the door.

While Richard pushed another trunk out. Penelope reached down and unlatched the older trunk before her. Inside were heavier clothes made of thick fabrics like velvet and fur. The scent of mothballs was strong. "It looks as though she was already storing her winter clothes away, but it's not even mid-February."

"And we just had a heavy snowfall only a few days ago. Most people wait until at least March to put away their winter clothes. We usually get at least one final good bit of frost early that month before spring fully sets in," Richard said, staring down at the clothes with a frown.

"True," Pen said, relishing the months when she could finally step outside without being weighed down by coats and winter wear. It seemed so far away, especially after the most recent heavy snowstorm. "Let's have a look inside the newer trunk."

She bent to unlatch and open it, already suspecting what she might find. Sure enough, the clothes inside were meant for warmer weather. That trunk didn't have the scent of mothballs.

"Well, this certainly speaks to an extended trip. But even with an unconfirmed holiday, she'd at least tell *someone* about it wouldn't she? Why be so circumspect about things? And where has she been for the past few days? To leave her dogs in such a state, I feel something is wrong."

"Yes, that's the odd thing. People are generally attached to their pets. I had a dog growing up."

"You did?" Pen said with a surprised smile, wondering why she was just now hearing about it.

"I suppose he was really my father's. Pip, a terrier, already almost seven years old by the time I was born. He sadly died when I was seven myself. If we didn't take him with us on a trip, we made sure to leave him with the neighbors."

"Well, I didn't know Mrs. Abernathy well enough that

she might call on me to care for Dot and Dash while she was gone. Especially if she was going away for such a long period as these trunks indicate. Maybe Alice was right and she planned on taking them with her."

"That still doesn't explain the past couple of days, or the dogs. I saw the mess in the kitchen. Some of it was them getting sick over something, maybe poisoning? Just how well do you know Mrs. Abernathy? Did she seem depressed?" Richard asked, a grim look on his face.

Pen knew exactly what he was hinting at. "I haven't really interacted with her all that much, only brief introductions when Cousin Cordelia and I moved in. I do know she's a widow. Her husband died about two years ago she said. To be fair, she didn't seem all that broken up about it. Besides, I doubt after all this time *that* would be the cause of her doing something so drastic. Maybe out of desperation, the dogs got into something they shouldn't have for food."

Richard didn't look entirely convinced, but nodded all the same. "Do you know if she had any relatives? Perhaps they might know something."

Pen thought back to the holiday dinner she'd hosted on Thanksgiving. Arabella had needed to borrow cream for the coffee from her neighbor across the hall. "Do you remember Arabella saying something about Mrs. Abernathy spending Thanksgiving with her nephew? She said it was unusual for her to spend the holiday with him, at least according to the cook."

Richard's brow lifted in appreciation. "That mind of yours never ceases to amaze me."

Penelope pursed her lips. "It was only three months ago. Still, there must be some contact information for him, somewhere. Let's wait for Alice to return and ask her."

In the meantime, they explored the apartment more in-depth. In the bedroom, she briefly noted the books on the bedside, *Women in Love* by D.H. Lawrence, which caused her to quirk an eyebrow, and *House of Mirth* by Edith Wharton, which Pen knew wasn't a romance at all. If anything it was the exact opposite, about a woman deliberately avoiding marriage.

She moved on to the gramophone and box of records. The record still set on the player was the French opera *Lakmé*. She quickly flipped through the other records which were mostly dance music, and quite the variety at that. Everything from the Venetian Waltz to La Cumparsita, which usually accompanied the Tango. To her surprise, there were also more modern selections like Tiger Rag, The Charleston, and shockingly, The Black Bottom Stomp. Pen only knew about the latter because she was close friends with Lucille Simmons, a jazz singer at the Peacock Club, and had heard it played on occasion there. Pen tried to imagine the diminutive older woman dancing the Charleston or the Black Bottom.

People could certainly surprise you. Working as a private investigator had told Penelope that much.

The second bedroom was perfectly nondescript, nice enough for a guest, but nothing special otherwise. In the library, Penelope was more thorough. There were yet more of the figurines that she had seen in the living room. In the middle of the library, there was a large table with a vase of hydrangeas and lavender, as fresh as the roses elsewhere were.

Bookshelves took up an entire wall. The case closest to the window held many leather-bound tomes, perfectly lined up, though the case was more than half-empty. Pen explored the titles, mostly authors like Herman Melville, Joseph Conrad, and Jack London. That seemed at odds with the romantic woman that the rest of the apartment seemed to hint at. It must have been her late husband's collection. Pen pulled one to discover it was a first edition, in perfect condition.

Moving on to the other cases, Penelope saw large art books that depicted lush, floral scenes, ballerinas, lovers, or anything else romantic. There were a lot of books dedicated to flowers. She picked up one: *The Victorian Language of Flowers*. She casually flipped through it to learn it was like a dictionary, explaining the meaning behind flowers.

Most of the higher shelves held classic romantic novels by Austen and Brontë, and poetry by Byron and Sappho (which was quite astonishing). There were also well-thumbed dime novel romances books that offered more purple or flowery prose as euphemisms.

Penelope smiled to herself, secretly congratulating Mrs. Abernathy for so shamelessly indulging herself. Now, *House of Mirth*, about a young carefree woman latching onto her free-spirited independence, made a bit more sense. Considering the fact that the case with books like *Heart of Darkness* was mostly empty, perhaps the good widow had finally been shedding the last remnants of her late husband's memory and enjoying her newfound independence.

Richard found her. "The good news is, it seems the dogs resorted to using the toilets to satisfy their thirst. At least that water would have been fresh. That's probably why they don't look worse than they do. Still, one has to feel for them and what they've been through the past few days."

"I suspected as much. Thank goodness for modern plumbing."

"Yes, if only dogs could be trained on how to use it. I thought about cleaning up their mess. There's a trash chute conveniently located just as you enter the kitchen. However, if they have been poisoned, the lab will want to test it—only if there's foul play at hand, mind you."

"So you think there might be?"

"This is all very strange, I'll admit. Still, it won't be a priority unless we find out she's dead."

They heard the front door open and the sound of happy dogs rushing into the apartment. Richard and Penelope walked out to greet Alice, who was flushed as the blood rushed to her happy yet frozen face.

"Alice, we thought perhaps a relative of Mrs. Abernathy's might know more about her plans. I know she has a nephew. Do you know him or how to get in contact with him?"

If anything, her face became a deeper shade of pink to the point of being red. The smile disappeared and her brown eyes hardened into cool slits, filled with contempt.

"Oh yes, I know a bit about Walter Abernathy."

CHAPTER FOUR

Richard and Penelope stared at Alice, both of them slightly taken aback by the normally cheerful attitude that had evaporated at the mention of Mrs. Abernathy's nephew.

"I take it you've met Walter Abernathy?" Pen asked.

"Well, no," Alice admitted, the icy look fading from her eyes. They lit up again with umbrage. "But I do know he has never cared about Mrs. Abernathy. He's the only family she has left and he never even visits her! She told me that he never approved of anything she did, particularly how she spent his uncle's money, even though he has plenty of money of his own."

She let out a puff of hot air, calming down. "I'm quite close with my younger sisters and my parents. I visit every weekend, even though they live in Fort Hamilton down in Brooklyn. It takes ages to get there. I even went this weekend, despite the slush and mud and snow. Some of the streets there aren't even paved yet, you know."

"So he probably wouldn't be someone she might confide in, say about her plans for a trip or moving?"

"He'd be the last person she'd tell about anything!"

Penelope did note that there were no photographs or portraits in the apartment at all. Even her late husband hadn't maintained a visual presence.

"Still, he is family, and you said her only living relative?" Richard asked. "So if something were to happen to her, he'd be in line to inherit everything."

"I suppose so, and isn't that just a shame? Though I can't see Mrs. Abernathy forgetting about Dot and Dash that way. I'll bet he doesn't even like dogs," she said with a firm set to her mouth.

"Does he live in New York?"

"Right near Wall Street, I believe. That's where he works. According to Mrs. Abernathy, that's all he does is work. He doesn't even have to."

"It seems as though you and she were close enough to chat about family?" Pen suggested.

"Oh yes, she was a lovely woman. She always had Martha make me a cup of coffee in the morning for us to enjoy together after I brought the dogs back."

"And yet she didn't tell you her plans? Why she had all her clothes packed? Where she was going Friday?"

Alice's face fell. "No. I just don't understand it. She would have told me if she was moving."

Richard and Penelope exchanged a glance.

"Had anything changed with regard to how she acted lately? Was she less talkative? Did she seem blue at all?" Richard asked.

"Oh no, if anything she seemed happier. I'd catch her humming songs to herself or playing them on her gramophone, and I'd even see her dancing a time or two. Since I've been working for her, she's been involved in interesting activities like art and dance and going to museums or gardens. And all these flowers she had sent to fill the apartment, they were coming far more frequently."

"Right," Richard said, the expression on his face matching Penelope's own confusion. "Well, I think we should at least talk with her nephew before jumping to any conclusions. Or perhaps someone who handles her affairs. You wouldn't happen to know who that is?"

"No, we never talked about that sort of thing. She hated to discuss anything business related."

"Perhaps her nephew would know. Do you have an address or number to call him?"

"No, but..." Alice rushed to the library. Richard and Penelope followed. She went to a desk with a rolling top and opened one of the side drawers. She rifled through and pulled out an envelope that had been opened. "She keeps most of her correspondence and other important papers here. His address is on the outside of this envelope."

Richard took hold of it and showed it to Penelope to commit to memory. It was an address in the financial district. Walter really did live close to where he worked.

"Do you mind coming with us, Miss Winterfort? You seemed to know Mrs. Abernathy better than anyone and you might be helpful."

"Of course. Certainly, you don't expect the worst though, do you? I can't see Mrs. Abernathy doing that."

"Let's not jump to conclusions just yet. First, we'll see what her nephew has to say."

CHAPTER FIVE

R ichard drove Alice and Penelope to Walter's apartment building. Cousin Cordelia had pleaded weariness and stayed behind, making sure to leave Penelope with the reminder that it had been due to spending all morning in church.

Penelope was far too invigorated with the prospect of a new mystery to solve. Under normal circumstances, she might have simply thought poor Mrs. Abernathy had suffered a slip and fall on the ice somewhere. But surely someone would have found her already?

Then there were Dot and Dash. To have left them alone for days? It spoke to some far worse misfortune, perhaps even foul play.

The apartment building where Walter lived was nice enough, though not nearly as well-set as the Alstonian. Still, it at least had a doorman who informed Detective Prescott that Mr. Abernathy had gone out. He begrudgingly suggested (only because a New York detective had asked) Mr. Abernathy might have gone to work as per usual on a Sunday to "get ahead of the markets."

As the daughter of a man in finance, Pen had an idea of what that meant from a practical standpoint. From a personal one, it spoke to a man who, much like her father, put money above all else, including social interaction. No wonder he and his aunt were so distant. She seemed to spend her days committed to enjoying life.

Penelope was glad that Richard had decided to come with them as the doors to the building where Walter worked were firmly locked. It took some knocking to get the attention of a recalcitrant security guard who took his time unlocking the doors for them.

"I need to speak to a Mr. Walter Abernathy who works at Schmidt & Co. Can you tell me if he's here and on what floor the offices are located?"

The guard shrugged. "If he works here, he has his own key to get in. I don't monitor all of the comings and goings. But Schmidt is on the third and fourth floors. You can access the offices on the third."

"Thank you," Richard said much more politely than Penelope would have.

They took the elevator up to the third floor. It opened to a small hall with a vacant receptionist desk behind locked glass doors. Once again Richard knocked, this time much longer before someone came to see what all the ruckus was.

The man who appeared was young-ish, about Penelope's age of twenty-five, and handsome in a bluenosed sort of way. Even on a weekend, presumably working alone, he was in a three-piece suit, and his light brown hair was perfectly parted and combed back in the modern, conservative way. Soft blue eyes surveyed them with cautious curiosity and mild irritation at having been interrupted. Pen noted the way they lingered somewhat as they landed on

Alice. They then widened with alarm at the appearance of Detective Prescott's badge.

He quickly unlocked the door. "What can I help you with, detective? Is there a threat in the building?"

"Are you Mr. Walter Abernathy?"

That only had his eyes widening even more. "Yes? Is there a problem?"

"It's about your aunt. We're trying to locate her."

Pen noted the mild exasperation that colored his expression.

"What has she done?" He asked in an apologetic tone.

Before Richard could respond, Alice went into a tirade.

"What has she done? So you automatically assume the worst of her. It's just as I thought. You don't care one lick about her. Has it occurred to you that she could be missing, or worse? She could very well be lying dead in a ditch somewhere wondering why her only living relative has spared no thought for her welfare, but I see you have time for work."

Walter's cheeks flushed slightly at the accusation. His surprise at the verbal assault softened into something approaching concern. "Has something in fact happened to her?"

"The last time anyone saw her was on Friday, leaving her apartment building."

"That's hardly cause for concern, is it? My aunt has been quite prone to flights of fancy since Uncle Spencer died. She may very well be in a hotel in New Haven or Boston, or, knowing her, perhaps even Florida or Cuba."

"She didn't have any luggage with her, save for a small valise, when the doorman saw her leave," Pen said.

"There is also the fact that she seems to have let go of her entire staff, and her clothes are all packed into trunks," Richard added.

"Well, there you have it. She probably has some sea voyage planned. Uncle Spencer left her a healthy sum of money. I assume you saw how she redecorated the apartment with it. Appalling." Of course a man would say that, though Pen did find the decor rather precious. "I'm surprised it's taken her this long to splurge on something far grander. As much as I may disapprove, I don't blame her for accommodating some of her wanton indulgences. Uncle Spencer wasn't a very...attentive husband in that regard. Still, I'm hardly in a position to know where she is or why she has left. The last time I even visited with Aunt Dorothy was at Christmas, the one time of year we visit. She certainly didn't inform me of her plans for the upcoming year."

"You were with her at Thanksgiving as well, which was unusual apparently?" Pen asked, remembering what Arabella had told her.

"Well...yes, that *was* unusual. I expected to spend Thanksgiving in the office again as I have since my parents died four years ago. She was kind enough to invite me to dinner last year. That's hardly suspect though. I imagine she's been lonely since Uncle Spencer passed, and probably sympathized with my loss. I'm her only relative as well."

"How terrible," Alice sympathized, her expressive face creasing with pity.

Walter blinked, looking slightly flustered. His cheeks colored again and he cleared his throat. "Yes, well, I do hope you find her. For all her faults, she was kind-hearted. I'm rather busy at the moment, but I would appreciate an update when you do find her, hopefully enjoying herself in some resort in a place with more enjoyable weather than we're presently having here in New York."

"What about her dogs?" Alice said.

"What of them?" Walter asked, looking bewildered.

"Well, she's not there to see to them. Surely you can take them in until we find out what happened to her? She wouldn't have left them to fend for themselves. A fact that *should* give you pause about her enjoying herself in some faraway place."

Walter looked as though she had asked him to parade through the streets in a toga while juggling live chickens.

"I'm sorry, who might you be?" He tried to make it sound nonchalant, even a bit pompous, but Pen could see the deep interest in learning more.

"Alice Winterfort. Mrs. Abernathy hired me to take care of Dot and Dash two times a day, but she let me go this past week."

"Well, I hereby re-hire you. Dot and Dash can stay with you, as I can hardly take them in. I'll double whatever she paid you."

"I can't keep them. My building doesn't allow dogs."

"Then they can stay at Aunt Dorothy's apartment and you come to feed and walk them."

"They'll get lonely!"

He gave her a look of consternation. "All the more reason I can't take them. I have a job and I haven't the foggiest idea how to keep dogs from being lonely."

"A little attention is all they need. Someone to scratch their ears and pet them, throw a stick or a ball for them to fetch."

His gaze softened with something like longing as she detailed the ways in which she doted on Dot and Dash.

"Also, there will be no one to walk them mid-day as I too have a job. I work at Macy's in the children's clothing department."

"Yes, well, I'm sorry, but I can't take the dogs, I simply can't."

"Zounds! I'll take Dot and Dash," Pen said, throwing up her hands. "I'll pay you to come by and walk them as usual, Alice, just As Mrs. Abernathy did."

Richard gave her an incredulous look, then smiled and shook his head in amusement. She simply shrugged, as though there was no other alternative.

"Oh, thank you, ma'am!" Alice cried.

"I insist you call me Penelope or Pen."

"Of course, thank you! I'll be by at eight o'clock in the morning as usual."

"Yes, I too appreciate it, er, Mrs...?"

"Miss Banks, but you can call me Penelope as well. I'm a private investigator. And now I suppose a temporary dog owner as well.

"Well, thank you, Miss Banks." Pen wasn't surprised he remained formal in addressing her. "It certainly saves me having to send them to the pound in Aunt Dorothy's absence."

"Oh, you horrible man!" Alice cried.

Walter blinked and looked stricken, then stumbled over his words. "I didn't mean—I just meant should the worst... well, it isn't that I would necessarily—"

"The good news is, the dogs will be safe and sound with me," Penelope gently interjected. She wondered just how safe and sound they *would* be in her apartment. Certainly, the cats might have something to say about it. "Now then, Mr. Abernathy, do you have an idea of who looked after Mrs. Abernathy's financial and legal affairs? I imagine she didn't handle it all on her own."

"Naturally. I would assume she remained with Mr. Franklin at Dunleavy & Patt, who handles all the Abernathy family financial and legal concerns." He gave their information.

"Will that be all then?"

"Yes, and thank you for your help," Richard said.

"Again, I'm sure she's fine. She'll probably be back tomorrow, realizing her mistake about the dogs."

"I certainly hope so...for their sake," Alice said in a censuring tone.

Walter's face was inscrutable as he stared back at her. "Yes, I agree. Well, good day."

They said their goodbyes and left him to his work.

"What an absolutely odious man," Alice said, her cheeks flushed and eyes bright.

"Handsome though," Pen mused, ignoring the surreptitious smirk Richard shot her. Cousin Cordelia wasn't the only one who accused her of being meddlesome.

"Handsome or not, he doesn't seem to care one fig about his aunt. And to put poor Dot and Dash into a pound." She huffed out a final bit of protest before once again thanking Penelope profusely for taking the dogs in.

"Let's check with this firm before we leap to any final conclusions regarding your neighbor. I imagine they won't be open on a Sunday, but I suppose with you so generously taking on the care of the dogs, one more day won't hurt."

"Unless she's been kidnapped—or worse," Pen pointed out.

"Exactly," Alice agreed. "Certainly it's worth searching the entire city in case she's right now clinging to life!"

Richard held up his hands in protest. "Ladies, ladies, right now, Mrs. Abernathy can only be classified as a missing person. All signs so far point to her intention to leave either permanently or for an extended period of time. Honestly, I've dedicated far more time to this than any other officer of the law would under such circumstances." He gave Pen a wry look. "Besides, Miss Banks here is a private investigator. I'm sure she already has plans to start snooping in my absence."

"Will you?" Alice pleaded.

"Yes, and it's hardly snooping if it's for her own welfare. If she is lying in a ditch somewhere, she'll be grateful for it. Alice, I hope you'll be willing to help me when we return. You might provide some useful insight."

"Oh yes, anything for Mrs. Abernathy."

Pen gave Richard a satisfied smile. He returned a look that told her what she already knew...she was probably in over her head with all she'd decided to meddle with on this case. Two dogs and a missing widow. He was probably also amused by her not-so-subtle attempt at playing Cupid a moment ago.

"You two do that. In the meantime, tomorrow I'll check with Dunleavy & Patt to see if they know anything about her plans or whereabouts. They'll also most likely be able to give me information about her staff so I can question them. Will that satisfy the both of you?"

Pen and Alice nodded their approval. "Hopefully this is all for naught and she really does turn up tomorrow."

CHAPTER SIX

Back at the Alstonian, Penelope and Alice returned to Mrs. Abernathy's apartment. Dot and Dash were thrilled to see Alice yet again in such a short period and wasted no time showing their appreciation by nearly attacking her. She laughed and firmly told them to sit, which they instantly obeyed.

For many reasons, Penelope hoped Mrs. Abernathy was indeed enjoying a short holiday somewhere.

"I suppose I should give the key to you, since you're her neighbor. If she does come back, and I hope she does, you can easily return it to her. I'll just come to collect the dogs at eight tomorrow from your apartment."

"Yes, I have a butler who can let you in. I'll let Chives know about our arrangement with Dot and Dash. Now then, I'd like to get a better picture of Dorothy Abernathy. Is there anything you can tell me? I see that she likes flowers, and these little figurines, Lachapelles, I understand?"

Pen walked over to the nearest one, sitting on a table that held a vase of fresh red roses. She picked up the figurine which was of a woman sitting underneath what looked to be a flowering Cherry Blossom tree. Her gaze was lowered to the bed of pink blossoms she sat atop. Pen looked at the bottom of the figurine to see "Lachapelle" printed in gold lettering. "It seems authentic."

"Yes, she collected them, always a new one every week. That's a recent one, or at least I haven't seen it yet, not that I pay too much attention to them. They are lovely, but a bit twee for my tastes and she has so many of them. It's a wonder Dot and Dash haven't broken at least one or two, but they are such good dogs." She turned to beam at Dot and Dash still obediently sitting near the wall.

"If they really are authentic, she must have had some plan for either delivering them or packing them away; perhaps even selling them?"

"Oh, she'd never sell them. They were far too dear to her."

"Well, that speaks to her being back soon," Pen said, if only to infuse some optimism into the situation. "I think perhaps we should take a look at that desk of hers. I know it's private correspondence, but...well, I won't tell if you don't."

"If it helps find out where she is, I'm fine with it," Alice said, leading the way into the library. Pen walked over to the desk and unceremoniously lifted the rolling top. The papers inside were mostly neat and orderly, filed chronologically.

"She certainly makes things easy. There are plenty of receipts here. Perhaps we can devise a timeline of her activities in the days before she left."

"That's a grand idea," Alice said cheerfully.

She and Penelope divided up the receipts, starting with the top. After a good thirty minutes, Pen began to note an obvious pattern.

"There are a few easily explainable one-off expenditures recently—a doctor visit, an appraisal for some valuables, several clothing stores. Of course, there are the usual bills one might expect, staff wages, utilities, and building maintenance. However, it seems, there are four places where she spent money on a weekly basis. As you pointed out, she did apparently purchase a weekly figurine from Lachapelle. Zounds, they cost more than I would have thought, though it's all within a certain range." There was no accounting for tastes, Pen thought, and it was Mrs. Abernathy's money to spend as she saw fit. She wondered what Walter might have had to say about it. Alice was being tactfully straight-faced at the amounts spent, though she had to be reeling.

Pen made a mental note to double the amount Mrs. Abernathy had been paying her to walk Dot and Dash.

"Then there was money both coming and going into an Aristotle Book Dealer." Pen's eyes rose to the half-empty bookshelf of rugged classics and figured that was where the incoming money was from. Mrs. Abernathy was slowly selling off her late husband's books. Perhaps that was where she had also obtained all the more romantic books on her shelves.

"Lashbrook Dance Studio, she was paying an awful lot every Thursday," Alice said, holding up a series of receipts. "But she did seem to love dancing, so it makes sense."

"For that amount, she was probably getting private lessons," Pen said, noting the payments. "Do you have a receipt for this past Thursday? Perhaps she confided in him about her Friday afternoon plans."

"No, the last one is from the week before. But it was snowing something awful this Thursday. She must have canceled. After all, she didn't even want me risking the trip here to walk Dot and Dash."

"Yes, well, at least we know what she was up to on Thursdays. Lachapelle was on Mondays. So, what did she do the other three days, most importantly, Friday? Eugene, our doorman, said she had been going out Friday afternoons and not returning during his shift."

"I don't know, but I'm just now noticing here there's a large cash payment of one thousand dollars to a Beau Blackman. It was paid only a week ago, but it doesn't say what for. It must have been something important if it was that much."

"Blackman?" Pen repeated. "That's the signature on the paintings in the living room, B. Blackman."

They both stood up and went back out to look at one of the paintings. It was of a small Tudor cottage with a thatch roof. Hydrangea bushes with fat flowers bordered the picket fence, beyond which was a garden with a variety of flowers. The scene was at twilight and the windows glowed with a warm, welcoming light. It was the kind of setting that made one want to disappear into it, which was no doubt why Mrs. Abernathy had so many done in similarly quaint settings. In the corner "B. Blackman" was scribbled in barely legible letters.

"It's a lovely painting, but hardly worth a thousand dollars, I would think," Penelope said staring at it with a critical eye. Agnes had taught her something about art, and any competent artist could recreate such a scene. Whoever Beau was, he had certainly taken advantage of poor Mrs. Abernathy, if she had paid a thousand dollars for that painting.

Pen pictured some prissy little man who probably thought modern art was a disgrace or, like some people, a sign of the downfall of civilization. Still, the images had apparently made Mrs. Abernathy happy, and that was all that really mattered. Again, it was her money to spend as she saw fit.

Penelope studied the painting. A name was hardly enough to go by in terms of finding out more about him. Still, she had to have gotten it framed somewhere. Pen reached up to lift the painting off its hooks. Like all the others it was about three feet wide and two feet tall. The ornate, scrolled frame was the heaviest part. It thunked on the floor and she leaned it against her legs to inspect the frame. There was no name for a shop. However, she did see a message written on the back of the canvas:

To Dorothy,
My petunia, my hope, my promise.
Love, B

"My petunia?" Pen said. Her image of the artist shifted from a fussy little man to an older, overly dramatic type.

"It could just be words of endearment from a close friend. Still, the message as a whole is a bit..."

"Yes, rather intimate," Penelope agreed. "Still, he wasn't just painting for her; they were obviously close. I think he might be a good place to start to learn more."

"It's already late, do you suppose any of the places from her receipts are open, especially on a Sunday?"

"I doubt it. But four leads are certainly not a bad start. We have the Lachapelle shop, the Aristotle Book Dealer, the Lashbrook Dance Studio, and now this Beau Blackman, artist extraordinaire."

Rather than hang the painting back up, Pen left it on the floor, leaning against the wall, with the message faced outward. She turned to Dot and Dash, still obediently watching them.

"I suppose it's time to move these two into their new home. I'm already exhausted thinking about it."

"Oh, don't worry, Dot and Dash are perfect angels. They shouldn't give you too much trouble."

"It isn't them I'm worried about."

CHAPTER SEVEN

"Have you gone perfectly mad, Penelope?" Cousin Cordelia exclaimed.

"It's just until we find Mrs. Abernathy," Pen said, pushing the large dog beds into a corner of the living room. Dot and Dash were sniffing around, probably becoming accustomed to the scent of their new abode. It wouldn't be quite as floral as Mrs. Abernathy's but, hopefully it would do.

Temporarily. Hopefully.

Pen certainly hoped her neighbor would return tomorrow, pleading a fit of absent-mindedness about her two pets. Cousin Cordelia was in a state.

"What about poor Lady Dinah? And your own cat? Did you consider their feelings?"

Lady Dinah was sitting in an armchair, tail lazily swiping back and forth as she looked on with absolute unconcern. Little Monster was sniffing the dog bed before deciding it would do as a perfect place to sleep.

"Oh no you don't," Pen said, picking him up and placing him back on the floor. She was more worried about Dot or

Dash being bullied into giving up their bed than anything they might do to him. He meowed his complaint before walking over to start a fight with one of them. Dot simply stared down with curiosity at the cat who was rapidly pawing at her leg. Fortunately, Little Monster eventually got bored and moved on.

"We should at least put the beds in a less conspicuous area. We still have the maid's quarters empty."

"We aren't pushing all the responsibility off on Chives or Arabella, Cousin. I'm paying Alice to come by twice a day. I can certainly handle them midday and for their last walk of the evening."

"And what if Mrs. Abernathy is...dead?" She whispered the last word, as though worried the dogs might hear.

"We'll concern ourselves with that when it happens." The last thing Pen wanted to do was send them to the pound, per Walter's suggestion.

"Oh Penelope, you never think these things through. My poor, precious Lady Dinah having her home invaded by two beasts."

"One would think she owned the place."

"Don't be rude, Penelope, she can hear you," Cousin Cordelia said, rushing over to pick up her white Persian, and stroke her fur.

"I'll find out what happened to Mrs. Abernathy soon enough. Alice and I already stumbled across several leads to work with tomorrow."

"Oh? What did you learn?" Her anger had instantly evaporated under the allure of potentially gossip-worthy information.

"She was taking an art class, and dance lessons it seems. Nothing too sordid."

"Oh," Cousin Cordelia said, disappointed. "Well, as for

Dot and Dash, they seem well-behaved enough, but I certainly hope you don't plan on having *me* take them out while you're at your little party tonight.

"Pineapples!" Pen had completely forgotten her friend's party. Benjamin "Benny" Davenport was hosting an anti-Valentine's Day bash that evening. She was hardly late; Benny's parties never really got going until the average New Yorker was tucked into bed, especially those who actually had to work for a living.

"See there? Already a disruption," Cousin Cordelia said, shaking her head.

"Applesauce, I'll walk Dot and Dash before I go, then quickly get dressed. You're still welcome to come," Pen teased.

"To a...*speakeasy*?" Again she whispered the word as though worried the pets might judge her for even knowing such a term. "And the theme itself? Who ever heard of an anti-Valentine's Day party? Who could possibly be opposed to love?"

"Someone who had married the wrong person," Pen said, thinking of Mrs. Abernathy and her husband Spencer. She thought of Benny. "Or just someone who can't be with the one they love, perhaps?"

"Nonsense, Benny shouldn't let such nonsense keep him from marrying. In these modern times, I'm sure his family will come around. Unless of course, it's some woman of ill repute he's interested in?" Once again, Cousin Cordelia's nose for scandal began twitching with avid interest.

She still hadn't caught on to Benny's proclivity when it came to love, and Pen wasn't about to travel down that avenue when she had a party to get dressed for.

"As far as I know, Benny has yet to find a young woman

he's interested in marrying, Cousin," she said, which was true enough.

"Well, he'll find someone soon. He's quite the catch—good breeding, handsome, and he dresses in such a debonaire way. If I were thirty years younger, and of course had never met my Harold, even I might be tempted. I feel such a connection with him."

"Well, he admires you as well," Penelope said, biting back a grin. "He'll be disappointed you didn't come."

"You'll just have to give him my regards, and perhaps a reminder that Prohibition is still very much in effect."

"Of course."

Despite the fact that Pen was very much in love with a certain detective, in defiance of the theme, she was rather looking forward to Benny's party. In fact, now that she thought about it, he and his like-minded friends might be of use to her with Mrs. Abernathy. Cousin Cordelia had made a very interesting point. It did seem as though men of Benny's persuasion and older wealthy women left to their own devices had quite a few things in common.

CHAPTER EIGHT

_____

As Cousin Cordelia had rightfully assessed, Penelope had deliberately slept in that morning. After all, if the Sabbath was good enough for God to take a rest, why not her?

The location of Benny's party was a private club (contrary to Cousin Cordelia's accusation of a speakeasy, though there would be enough illegal giggle juice to supply one) and the dress code was "Glad Rags & Costumes."

Particularly since it was hosted by Benny, Pen knew the guest list would include outcasts of every ilk, but only the swell kind. Thus, she wasn't surprised to see Lulu there, who was a fascination for every eye at the party, and not just due to race. She most certainly had a presence about her.

Pen had chosen a soft pink number that almost matched the walls of Mrs. Abernathy's apartment. Lulu had gone with a more daring red silk. Even amid men and women in absurd costumes, she couldn't help but draw attention just by wearing a dress.

"I don't have to introduce you two sinners," Benny

greeted with a coy smile. He was dressed like Louis XIV, with an outrageous wig and a period costume of pastel pink and blue brocade. He'd even grown a tiny little mustache.

"Funny you should say that, this place reminds me of Reverend Johnson's office at church," Lulu said, looking around at the oak paneling and sturdy furniture uncertainly.

"You didn't tell me you were a church girl, Lulu, dove. I would have dressed as something more...*tempting*," Benny said with a waggle of the eyebrows.

"Behave, you two," Pen teased. Looking around, good behavior was the last thing likely to happen that night. There were men dressed as women, women dressed as men, and at least one person dressed as both at the same time. A young man dressed as Cupid wore nothing but a loin cloth and curly blond wig, and a woman dressed as Eve wore even less, though a long-haired wig and a strategically placed fig leaf saved her a modicum of modesty.

It was probably for the best that Jane Pugley, Penelope's partner at the private investigation business where she worked, was in Poughkeepsie visiting her family with her fiancé, Alfred Paisley. While Jane had certainly become more worldly over the past year, she still probably would have gawped at the sight before her.

"Speaking of sin, where do I get one of those?" Pen asked, pointing to the glass of pink champagne in their hands.

Benny looped an arm through each of their arms and led them to the bar. "Tell me, dove, are you working on any scandalous cases? I've been terribly bored by New York society so far this winter."

"I may have an interesting missing person case. It's

someone who lives in my building." Pen didn't want to give too much away, in case Mrs. Abernathy wasn't in fact missing and didn't want her personal affairs aired to strangers.

"Go on," Benny said, as Pen took the flute of champagne graciously offered to her.

"She was a widow in her late fifties."

"Wealthy, I presume? Please tell me there is a pit of viperous relatives just waiting to get their fangs into her money."

"No, just a nephew who seems to have money of his own, and very little interest in her otherwise."

Benny's lower lip protruded with disappointment. "Any scheming household staff? Secret lovers? Immoral lawyers or accountants?"

"Hmm, the staff has disappeared, though I suspect they were just let go, probably on good terms. Tomorrow, we'll find out about her legal and financial advisors, but I have a sneaking suspicion that won't be fruitful. Old money and longtime relationships, and all that jazz. As for secret lovers well, that's the one big mystery, and probably where the answer lies."

"How very apt! The perfect thing for the theme of this party—done in by a secret lover. King Louis knew a thing or two about secret lovers," he said with a smirk as he gestured to his costume. "Though, I suppose his weren't all that secret."

"But did King Louis have the same taste in, ahem, fruit, that you do?"

Benny hissed at Lulu, curling his fingers like claws, then they both laughed.

"You two," Pen said in rebuke, though she couldn't keep

from laughing as well. One of the things she enjoyed about both Benny and Lulu was their frank disregard for social niceties. If there was ill repute to be discussed, those two didn't blush.

"Yes, yes, allow me to show you two off." Benny circled them around the room introducing them like two beloved pets, each of whom knew a fun trick to regale his guests with. Penelope didn't mind, as she found them equally fascinating. Lulu didn't mind because she adored attention, and they seemed to adore her insouciant retorts.

However, it was no surprise when business finally poked its way into the conversation. Pen was in a corner with Lulu, Benny, and three others, a man dressed as a Spanish bullfighter in a rather ornate traje de luces (Pen had spent a reckless year in Spain becoming quite acquainted with the local flavor), another in a court jester outfit, and Eve.

"She seemed to have a regular weekly schedule. Mondays she'd make a purchase of a Lachapelle figurine."

"Ugh, once upon a time my grannie simply couldn't stop buying those dear little things. With each one, I saw my inheritance getting smaller and smaller. I don't know what it is about them, but whoever that Lachapelle is, he certainly found his con," the bullfighter said, frowning.

"It's all about the image, don't you know. If you make something seem priceless, it becomes so," Benny said.

"Fortunately, she saw reason a couple of years ago; stopped buying them completely, out of the blue. Thank God! As for that ridiculous shop, you know you can't just walk into the store? It's all by appointment only. I think that's how he lures rich women in. It's that special attention he lays on them," he said with a wicked smile.

"Well, there you have it, Pen. Your secret lover," Lulu said with a laugh.

"I don't know, a man who deals in dainty china figures?" Eve asked doubtfully. Pen had to agree that the picture in her head didn't present the sort of dashing man Mrs. Abernathy would find in her sweeping romance novels.

"One never knows. I, of course would be able to tell you in an instant just from one conversation with the man. And now I'm rather intrigued," Benny mused. "Oh, do take me along when you interrogate him, Pen."

"I suppose I'll have to make an appointment first, it seems."

"Who are the others on this weekly list of lovers?" The jester asked.

"I don't know that they're *all* lovers," Pen said, her eyes widening at the thought. "That would be exhausting for anyone."

"Speak for yourself, dove," Benny teased.

"Pen only has enough fuel for one man," Lulu added.

"There's a lot of that going around it would seem," Benny said, pursing his lips her way. Lulu scowled back at him, and Pen was left in the dark, wondering to what they were referring. Though it did strike a note...something to return to later.

"At any rate, she also spent money at Aristotle's Book Dealer, though I suspect she was trading in her late husband's books for something a bit more...thrilling. She likes romances."

"Blah, next," Benny said, causing the jester and toreador to laugh.

"I like romances," Eve said with a pout.

"Of course you do, dove. Heaven knows Adam was

never the romantic type. You should have stuck with the snake, he would have been much more fun," Benny said, making her giggle.

"She liked dancing. Had quite the record collection, and it wasn't just waltzes. Someone was teaching her the Black Bottom Stomp."

That was enough to cause everyone to stare back at Pen in surprise.

"Well, there's your lover, honey," Lulu purred with a devilish smile.

"And then some," Eve of all people said, still looking skeptical.

"Who's to say a woman in her late fifties can't enjoy modern music and dance?"

Lulu leaned in. "I'll tell you what it is, this missing woman of yours finally put her husband in the ground and now gets to enjoy life without that little handcuff on her finger. Hell, she might have won one of those silly little dance marathons that are all the rage and is probably recovering in the booth of a speakeasy somewhere."

"Zounds, Lulu," Penelope said, picturing that ridiculous scenario. "Though, there is a grain of truth in some of what you said, I suspect. She would go out Fridays, and presumably stay out all night. This past Friday she had a valise with her."

That had them all atwitter, uttering the most sinful and colorful ideas.

"Really, we shouldn't gossip so. She left her dogs in a state, with no food or water for days. I suspect the worst," Pen said with a frown.

"You said there were four possible places? What was the fourth? We'll find your little Miss Independence," the jester said.

"An artist. She commissioned paintings by him, cozy little floral settings and cottages in the forest or by bubbling brooks. His name is Beau Blackman. If the paintings are anything to go by, I have an idea of what he probably looks like. Still, it seems they had some kind of personal relationship, so I'd really like to find him and speak with him."

"Beau Blackman," hummed the toreador. "That name is familiar. Jefferson goes to that art school. I think he mentioned him." He raised an arm and called out the name. A man dressed in a basic tuxedo walked over, though Pen caught a glimpse of wild, purple paisley print in the lining when he took a sip from his glass of champagne.

"Jefferson, you know Beau Blackman, the artist. He was teaching that class you took a year ago."

"Oh, yes," Jefferson said, raising an eyebrow. "It was... quite the experience."

"Pen here suspects he may have murdered someone!"

"I didn't say that," Pen protested, making the toreador laugh.

"Well, if he did kill her, she probably died happy. The man was a wonder when it came to helping me focus on my art."

"Does he still teach? I'd like to talk to him."

Jefferson laughed in an ambiguous way. "It was the Grand Central School of Art. He was a substitute when I attended, and I don't know what his schedule is these days. I've heard he's doing the life drawing class tomorrow morning, so it's best to catch him then. I'd like to go myself if only to reminisce," he said with a smirk.

"Life drawing? Well, that's quite the shift from what I saw. I suppose he's rather versatile."

"One can only hope!" Jefferson sang in a way that made Benny and his friends laugh.

Pen didn't need to work too hard to interpret that. Even Lulu smirked. It seemed Beau Blackman, wasn't the stuffy little man she had imagined him to be.

My, my, Mrs. Abernathy, what have you been up to? Pen thought to herself.

CHAPTER NINE

The next day, Penelope arrived at the office feeling grumpy and hungover. Alice had arrived that morning, as cheerful as ever, to take Dot and Dash out. Rather than tire them out, it had only made them more excitable when they returned. That had gotten Cousin Cordelia in a state, which meant poor Chives was more put upon than usual. Even her "medicinal brandy" couldn't settle the nerves of Pen's cousin.

"I'll return midday to walk them myself," Pen had promised. Considering the carpenters pounding away in her head—she should have stuck to gin at the party, as champagne always went straight to her head—she could only imagine how torturous that would be. Perhaps Cousin Cordelia had had a point about taking them on.

"I take it the party last night was a success?" Jane said cautiously as Pen sat at her desk, a cup of black coffee already to her lips.

"We have a new case," Pen said, her eyes still closed against the light coming through the windows.

"We do?" Jane perked up in pleased surprise. "What is it?"

"My neighbor's gone missing."

"Oh no."

"I'm sorry, I should have asked how your weekend with your parents went," Pen said, finally lifting her head to give Jane a preemptively sympathetic look.

Jane sighed. "I honestly don't understand why Alfred still wants to marry me. They were positively horrible to him. But he was nothing but perfect as usual."

"That's the sign of a good man. We can't choose our parents, but it's you he's marrying, not them. All the more reason for you to stay right here in New York with Alfie."

"Yes," she said brightening up. "But, um, how *was* the party? I've never been to one that Benny has hosted."

"Well...it certainly would have introduced you to some of New York's more *eclectic* elements. But the good news is, we're going out this morning! Have you ever been to the Grand Central School of Art?"

"There's an art school at Grand Central?"

"Yes, it opened only three years ago. And what a magnificent use of space! It seems my neighbor, Mrs. Dorothy Abernathy was a patron and friend of one of the artists who teaches there. I've been told we can find him teaching the life drawing class this morning. We should probably go now, if it's a morning class then he's—"

Pen heard the front door to the office open. Jane's desk was closer to the door leading to the outer office, so she scurried out to greet the potential client. Pen heard the unmistakable sound of Benny's voice.

"Jane! Here's hoping you are feeling more chipper than I am," he said, breezing in to greet Pen. He gave her a pout.

"Shame on you for pulling me out of bed at this ungodly hour."

"You're always welcome to go back to bed and be one of the idle rich again." She grabbed her purse and walked over to kiss the air beside his cheek. "We're headed out to the art school to meet this Beau Blackman."

"Ah yes, lover number one."

"I'm sorry?" Jane said, giving him a quizzical look.

"I'll explain on the way there, Jane. And we don't know for certain he's a lover. Right now, just a very close friend who made art for her. Come, let's go if we want to catch him."

———

The ride to Grand Central was long enough for Pen to explain everything to Jane, and thus give Benny all the details she had left out the night before.

"So you've taken on two dogs now? Really Pen, at this point just open up a zoo for pets of the deceased."

"We don't know she's deceased. In fact, I'm hoping her nephew was right and she simply went away for the weekend and, in some addle-headed mistake, just forgot about Dot and Dash." As much as Pen liked that scenario, if only for the dogs' sake, at this point, she wasn't hopeful. Perhaps Richard would discover something from her representative at Dunleavy & Patt, or at least get in touch with her staff.

Pen knew that she would have several trips to make that Monday, as such, she had incorporated the services of her chauffeur, Leonard, rather than try to catch taxis all over town. He dropped them at the entrance to Grand Central.

"It's on the seventh floor. I went to the exhibit for John

Singer Sargent after he died last year," Pen said as they entered.

The three of them navigated their way through the crowded main floor to find the elevators in the east wing. They got on and took them all the way to the top where the galleries and the school were located. Penelope was the one to speak to the young lady at the desk.

"Hello, we're looking for a Beau Blackman? I believe he teaches art here? Is the life drawing class still taking place? We haven't missed him, have we?"

"Yes, the life drawing class is actually just finishing," she said, giving Penelope an odd look. She probably wasn't used to the general public coming to inquire about the school rather than the gallery itself. She gave them directions, which took them past the galleries.

Pen figured the class ended at the top of the hour, which gave them ten minutes to briefly explore the art on display. With the fountains and trees, it almost looked like an indoor terrace. They didn't linger too long, all of them wanting to make sure they didn't miss Beau, should he end class early.

They found the door to the life drawing class closed and Pen put her ear to it. She strained to hear anything and pressed in closer. She was startled when the door suddenly opened and she fell into a student who was leaving early. He was just as surprised when they both toppled inward.

The soft sound of pencils and charcoal against paper ceased as all eyes turned toward the door. Jane and Benny stood in the doorway looking embarrassed. Pen was far more mortified as she quickly scrambled to her feet, offering to help the young man she'd inadvertently accosted. He flashed a tight smile and waved her hand away, standing up on his own.

The teacher frowned at them. "Can I help you?"

Pen offered an apologetic smile as she studied him. He was an older man, perhaps also in his fifties, with graying hair and a stern frown. There wasn't anything particularly handsome about him—certainly not enough to warrant the sort of titters she'd heard last night. Still, she supposed someone Mrs. Abernathy's age might find him a suitable companion.

"Yes, I was hoping to speak with you—after your class is done, of course. I didn't mean to barge in this way."

"It's my fault, I was leaving early," the student said, offering an apologetic wave as he rushed out.

"You're here now," he said in an exasperated tone. "Just wait quietly while my students finish. No need to deprive them of their final moments, despite the *rude* interruption."

"Of course," Pen said, making sure to look appropriately abashed.

In fact, her attention had been snatched by the model on display, sitting on a stool, with his back slightly twisted. He was nude, of course. With that much of him so prominently on display, she couldn't find a single flaw. He had long, dark hair, almost down to his mid-back, making him look like some romantic hero from centuries earlier. It was such a unique feature, it only made him seem rebellious and daring in an age where few young men let their hair grow past the collar. Pen felt her stomach flutter just a bit. He was ruggedly handsome as well, with full lips that probably easily curled into a smile, a bladed nose, and a level brow. He was extremely well-toned, with prominent muscles on display, which certainly gave the students plenty to work with.

That, of course, didn't factor in the most prominent part of him on display.

Pen tried to force her mind into that of a student,

studying a model, or perhaps a nurse, looking at a patient. Anything to make it seem less provocative. It was almost impossible, and she could see why several of the female students had a bit of color in their cheeks even as their pencils and bits of charcoal slashed away at the paper in front of them.

"*Hello*, David," Benny murmured next to her, just as mesmerized by the model. "Though, I think Michelangelo would have needed a bit more marble with this one."

Pen silently elbowed him, biting back a laugh. She turned her attention to Jane, whose face was as red as a beet. Her cornflower blue eyes were like saucers as she stared at the man, who showed not an ounce of self-consciousness.

"Alright," the teacher said with an aggrieved sigh. "I suppose that's all for today. Hopefully, you weren't too distracted toward the end." He turned to give the intruding trio a harsh look. All three of them lowered their eyes with overt apology.

The students seemed to deflate all at once, their shoulders relaxing and postures becoming less rigid as they closed their pads and put away their pencils and charcoal. The model stood up, shamelessly stretching out his back, perfectly unconcerned as to what he was boldly displaying. Pen had the sneaking suspicion he enjoyed the minor commotion he caused among the fairer sex, trying not to be too blatant in their ogling.

One stayed behind specifically to chat with him, a kittenish smile plastered on her face. His grin was no less flirtatious as he shrugged into his robe.

"Can I help you?"

Pen tore her eyes away from the model and the student, and turned to greet the teacher. "Yes, my name is Penelope

Banks, and I'm a private investigator. I was hoping to talk with you about Dorothy Abernathy?"

"Who?"

"Well...you painted a few works for her, cottages and flower gardens, things like that?"

He looked at her as though she were an idiot. "As you can plainly see, I work with the human figure. You must have the wrong person."

"Mr. Blackman, I can assure you that—"

"Actually, I'm Beau Blackman."

All eyes turned to the model who was finally decent in his robe. He offered Pen a curious smile as he gathered his long, lush hair up into a loose bun at the back of his head, held in place with a thin strap of leather. For some reason that only made him more appealing. Next to her, Jane inhaled deeply and sighed out something that sounded like a small moan.

"Good for you, Mrs. Abernathy," Benny breathed out under his breath.

"*I'm* Theodore Kunen. Beau was gracious enough to model for the class today. I suppose he must earn his keep somehow," the teacher said in a dry tone. "I assume I'm not needed then?"

"No, thank you. I apologize for my disruptive entrance. We just wanted to ask Mr. Blackman a few questions."

"He does seem to be the man of the hour. I'll leave you to it. Thank you for assisting today Beau."

"It was my pleasure, Theodore."

Theodore snorted, gave him a smirk, and left.

"I apologize for interrupting your, er, session," Pen said to Beau. The student next to him studied her with cool eyes. "I was told you were a teacher here."

"I am, oils mostly, and usually still life, but I accommodate the patron's request. You were asking about Dorothy?" He turned to the student. "I'll chat with you later, after this."

She seemed reluctant to go, but sighed and nodded. She made sure to give Pen one last hard, possessive stare before leaving.

"You did a number of paintings for her?" Penelope continued.

"I did. Those kinds of settings are not my usual subject, but again, what the patron wants, I must accommodate. Even the masters had to pay the bills with commissioned works. I've been introducing her to more, *ahem*, sophisticated art. Have you heard of an artist named Georgia O'Keeffe? Dorothy was particularly intrigued with her *Grey Line With Black, Blue And Yellow*."

"Yes, I have heard of that one," Pen said, knowing full well that the painting in question had caused a bit of stir with its representation of a flower. She had the feeling Beau was being deliberately provocative, which she was certain Mrs. Abernathy wouldn't appreciate.

Beau laughed softly. "Yes, Dorothy was beginning to appreciate modern art in all its forms."

"I'm actually here because it seems she's gone missing."

His handsome face creased with concern. "Missing?"

"She was last seen on Friday and hasn't been back all weekend. She's my neighbor you see."

"You live at the Alstonian?" He stared at Pen with more interest.

"Yes, right across the hall from her. Her two dogs, Dot and Dash, were left alone for days. I'm taking care of them now. Still, I don't think she would do that to them unless something was wrong."

"No, she loves those dogs," he said, his eyes dropping to the floor in thought.

"Did she tell you of any plans she had for an extended trip? Or perhaps she was moving away from New York City?"

"In a manner of speaking. She was going to Europe for the year."

"She told you that?" Pen asked in surprise.

"Yes, in fact she invited me to join her."

"Really?"

"Yes, but I had to decline. I adore Dorothy, but I've just accepted a position here. Teaching is my passion."

"Right," Pen said, wondering how to address the burning question that was on her mind.

Beau studied her with a slow grin. "You're wondering what my relationship with Dorothy was?"

"It had crossed my mind," she breathed out, grateful he had been the one to bring it up.

"Yes, we were more than an artist and patron, teacher and student." Again, he stated it in the most provocative way, hinting at something sordid. Jane inhaled sharply and Benny chuckled. Beau's grin spread even more, completely unashamed. "She was a very passionate woman. That's why she invited me to join her in Europe. But you say she's gone missing? Are you sure she hasn't already left?"

"Her trunks are still sitting in her apartment. And what about her dogs? At this point, I fear the worst."

"I see," Beau fell onto one of the student's stools, the look of concern returning to his face as he concentrated on the floor in front of him.

"Was she upset when you declined? Was she...lonely?"

"Lonely?" He lifted his gaze questioningly. "You don't think she...?" He chuckled and shook his head. "No,

Dorothy was anything but lonely. I shouldn't say it, but if it helps find out what happened to her, then I hope she won't mind. I wasn't the only man she...entertained."

"Oh," Pen said, tactfully. "Do you have a name?"

He shrugged. "She never told me names. Except there was one, an Alan?"

"Lashbrook?"

He shrugged. "I didn't know his last name. She took dance lessons with him. I had the impression it was more than just classes with him as well."

"I see." Penelope was learning far more about her neighbor than she really wanted to, but it did explain things. She wondered if Mrs. Abernathy's bluenosed nephew knew about any of this. She was doubtful. "Did she ever discuss Lachapelle, or a book dealer named Aristotle?"

"Lachapelle," he repeated, as though it struck a note but he couldn't place it.

"The figurines she collected."

"Ah, yes, those little things," he chuckled and shook his head. He became serious again at Pen's expression, reminding him why she was there. "I just know she liked them, is all. She dedicated her Mondays to visiting that shop. I'm not sure for how long, or if there was anything more to it. As for books, I only know what she liked to read. That was another area where she was...expanding her horizons, so to speak. She was particularly fond of flowery passages. She was, quite frankly, a bit obsessed with flowers. She wanted to leave in time to see Paris once spring set in."

"Do you know where she may have been going this past Friday?"

He shook his head no and shrugged. "Sorry."

"So, you weren't the one to send her flowers?"

"Flowers?" He seemed confused.

"The roses in her apartment?"

He chuckled and shook his head. "The only flowers I sent her were of the painted variety."

"Right, just one final question. She seems to have given you a rather large sum recently, a thousand dollars?"

His brow rose in surprise.

"I'm working with a detective and we naturally searched her belongings. She had a receipt for cash given to you."

"Yes," he said, giving her a wary look. "That was a parting gift. Her way of saying goodbye. Dorothy was a very generous woman. I do hope you find her."

"I do too."

"I should probably get dressed. It's getting rather chilly."

"Of course," Pen said with a wry smile before leaving with Jane and Benny.

"That was...interesting," Jane said hesitantly once they were back in the gallery area.

"I believe titillating is the word you're looking for, dove," Benny said with a smirk."Or perhaps stimulating?"

Jane's violent blush was a firm reminder that it was a good thing she hadn't gone to Benny's party the night before.

"At least now we know why she let go of her staff and had those trunks packed. If she wanted to reach Paris before spring began, it makes sense to leave in February. That still doesn't explain where she went Friday, or why she hasn't come back."

"Um, what did he mean by that Georgia O'Keeffe painting? Is it...scandalous?" Jane asked, avid curiosity written all over her face.

"That depends on your view of...flowers," Benny said, smirking.

"Don't tease, Benny, we're on a case."

"Yes, my very first officially working with you! This is rather more fun than I thought it would be."

"Jane, I'll show you a postcard of the painting at some point. For now, we really need to meet with these other men. I think Mr. Lashbrook is the next person we should talk to, based on what Beau said. But first, I need to go home and walk Dot and Dash, then talk to Richard and see if he's learned anything from Mrs. Abernathy's attorneys or former staff."

CHAPTER TEN

"**W**e've found her body."

Penelope was already taut in anticipation of what news Richard might have had for her. Even though she had been expecting such an update, it still made her go even more rigid as she held onto the phone's receiver.

Fortunately, Cousin Cordelia was out at one of her social charity luncheons. Pen was happy to wait until the end of the day to give her the news, when she wouldn't object to a little tipple to calm her easily frayed nerves.

She looked down at Dot and Dash who looked up with eyes filled with eagerness to go on their walk. As though sensing something was wrong, one began to whine. The pink collar indicated it was Dot. Dash's was lilac.

"What happened?" Pen asked, sagging into the chair next to the phone in the hallway of her apartment.

"She was strangled apparently. The autopsy will say for sure, but the external signs are there."

"My God," Pen said, instinctively bringing her hand up to her neck. "Where did they find her?"

"In the park, not too far from your apartment, if you can

believe it. Whoever killed her took the time to bury her under a snow drift that only melted enough last night to reveal her body. The long white fur coat didn't help things. It was actually the owner's dog who first sniffed her out."

"Did she have her jewelry on? According to Eugene, she was wearing her nice pieces. Also, she would have had a valise with her."

"No, both were missing. I don't see our murderer trying to bury the valise with her. He probably rifled through it to take anything valuable and dumped the rest somewhere. I'm not too hopeful about finding it. As for her jewels, we'll be checking in all the usual places, jewelry stores, estate shops, and some less-than-upstanding establishments."

"You aren't treating this as a simple murder as a result of robbery, are you?"

"No, but I'm not ruling it out either. She was found in the east side of the park not too far from where you live, the area just before you get to the zoo."

Pen considered that. It really was quite close to where they lived. "So someone may have lured her there as soon as she left the building. Friday, it would have still been fairly wet and snowy. Then again, she was getting a taxi, Eugene said. So perhaps she had been killed on her way home? He let it slip that she usually returned on Saturday morning. I need to find out where she was going these past few Fridays." Pen paused. "Unless you object of course?"

"A wealthy widow murdered in Central Park, within viewing distance of some of the city's most prominent homes and apartments? We'll take all the help we can get on this one Penelope. But if my superior asks, you didn't hear me say that."

Pen smiled. "I'll be very discreet, Richard. I assume you've been in touch with Dunleavy & Patt?"

"Naturally. Apparently, she was planning an extended trip abroad. She had instructed them to transfer some of her funds to several banks in Europe in preparation. She had also purchased two first-class tickets on the S.S. Fairway leaving in a few weeks."

"Two? I suppose she found a replacement for Beau Blackman, the artist."

"Beau Blackman?"

Penelope told him about her adventures that morning, not leaving anything out. "He couldn't have been much older than I am."

"I'm sure that caused a stir for both Jane and Benny, for entirely different reasons."

"It caused quite the stir for me as well," she teased.

"Do I need to worry?"

"I would never object to you ogling an attractive woman who was perfectly nude in front of you, darling. A robust libido is a healthy thing in a relationship."

"Libido?"

"I read it in a journal once. It means—"

"I know what it means," he said, laughing. "I suppose a well-rounded education is important as well. How would I keep up with a wife who remembers everything she reads?"

"I'll educate you, darling. This case has me feeling rather *robust* as it is, or perhaps lacking. It seems Beau wasn't the only object of Mrs. Abernathy's affection. In fact, I was planning on visiting Mr. Lashbrook at the dance studio this afternoon."

"Need I remind you to be careful? We are dealing with a murder case now."

"I'll have my little jade gun with me."

"That doesn't reassure me."

"Even with the practice I've put in?"

"Just, take Jane and Benny with you again. I can't believe I'm saying it, but at least that will give me some comfort."

"Three against one is always good odds."

He laughed. "Let me know what you find out, especially before you do anything...reckless."

"When am I ever reckless?"

"Should I answer that?"

Pen pursed her lips. "Alright, but it usually pays off, no?"

"Rather than encourage you with an answer, I'll hang up now and get back to working on this case."

"Wait, did you find out about her staff?"

"Ah, yes, she dismissed her maid and cook, Sally and Martha, both with glowing letters of reference and a sizable parting gift of money. According to her attorney, their last day was Friday."

"Friday? Then what did she have planned for Dot and Dash? There was no one to feed or see to them this past weekend. She had already let Alice go."

"Yes, that is odd. If she was planning to leave them behind, she should have at least taken them to the pound."

"Which she wouldn't have done. I think, wherever she was going, she planned on taking them with her. Did you get a name for the service that the maid and cook were hired from or returned to? Unless they already found new employers?"

"I'm already planning a trip to have a chat with them, if only to learn more about Mrs. Abernathy's plans and who she may have been meeting on Friday. Considering the circumstances of her murder, I'm not inclined to suspect either of them did it. It's rare for a woman to strangle another woman. It takes quite a bit of strength and force. I believe it was a man."

"Well, there seems to be no shortage of men in this case. I'm going to continue to look at the ones in her life."

"Again, be careful, Penelope, and please let me know what you find, especially if you feel you're on the path to danger."

"Of course, detective," she said with a smile. "But right now I feel another murder coming on if I don't take Dot and Dash out."

Upon hearing their names, the dogs' ears perked up and they began whining. Richard and Pen said their goodbyes and she quickly found their leashes to take them out as originally planned. Rather than take the main elevator, she detoured toward the service elevators, which would be quicker. Pen made a mental note to use them in the future if she was ever in a hurry.

The side service door let them out on 69th Street. The two dogs already knew which way to go, tugging her toward 5th Avenue. As soon as the signal allowed, they practically dragged her across the street in a rush, and through the small entrance to Central Park.

That part of the park, north of the zoo, was mostly rambling paths and small hills, surrounded by trees. Other than a few children playing in what was left of the snow, there weren't many people around. No one to hear Mrs. Abernathy scream if she had been in danger.

They soon came upon a police barricade and an officer preventing the public from straying off the path into a tree-dotted small hill. Pen could easily see how someone could lure Mrs. Abernathy into murder there, even something as involved as strangulation. It was well away from the walking path and well hidden by the barren branches and tree trunks. Her body must have been hidden on the other side of the small rise. That would have blocked her from the view of the park paths. The wall on the other side would have blocked her from view of the sidewalk and street. Even looking down from the Alstonian, she would have been hidden by the trees. No wonder it had taken so long to find her.

"Poor Mrs. Abernathy," Pen said to herself, realizing she had died so close to home. "Who lured you out here?"

It would definitely have had to be someone she knew.

Dot and Dash both let out a small whine, as though noting that was where their mistress had died. Perhaps it was some strange perception they had. The three of them stood there, silently acknowledging her loss.

"Please move along ma'am," the police officer said. Pen didn't argue with him, and led the dogs on.

Once they had done their business and finally seemed to tire out, she led them back toward 69th Street. While they waited for the light to change, she stared at the front entrance to the Alstonian. She frowned in thought, so deeply into her own head she didn't realize the cars had finally stopped to allow them to cross.

Pen rushed to the other side of the street and went through the front entrance. It was afternoon, which meant Eugene was on duty again. His eyes went wide at the sight of the dogs, but he didn't protest them coming through the front, since it was a resident leading them.

"Eugene, when you saw Mrs. Abernathy leave, you said she was catching a taxi? Did you see her actually get into one?"

"Well, no," he said after thinking for a moment. "But I assume she did, since she crossed the street. I figured one had stopped for her and idled on the park side of the street.

I got distracted by a resident before seeing whether or not she actually got into a taxi."

5th Avenue was a one-way street that only went south. It was possible she had gone up to 69th and crossed to get a cab that was idling closer to the park. Or perhaps she had crossed for another reason?

Pen turned to look out the glass front doors to make sure Eugene couldn't view the entrance to the park from his desk. "So she could have entered the park instead?"

"Why would she have done that?" He gave her a bewildered look.

"Never mind. Just to be clear, you didn't actually see her get into a taxi."

"No, I guess I didn't."

"Thanks, that's helpful. Also, you said she had on nice jewelry that day. Do you remember what it was?"

"Boy do I ever. It was that diamond necklace, the one with the blue stones, what do they call 'em?"

"Sapphires?"

"Yeah, that sounds right. It kind of looked like an upside-down crown, you know the kind women wear, with all the jewels and things. Must have had at least fifty stones in it. You could see them glittering all the way from my desk. I thought about warning her to pull her coat closed over them, but I guess women like to show that kind of thing off."

Pen left that alone. Still, she did recognize the necklace. She'd seen Mrs. Abernathy wear it once. It was impressive enough for Pen to get caught staring at it, which led to a brief discussion about them.

"A woman should always wear her most expensive jewelry when she's happy, preferably diamonds. A gift from my husband, when we first married. I don't think he'd appreciate the rendezvous I'm wearing them to this afternoon," Mrs. Abernathy had said with a conspiratorial laugh.

Pen hadn't needed any interpretation for that. Had Mrs. Abernathy been off to meet that same man the past Friday?

"Say, why all the questions? Did you learn anything?" Eugene asked, drawing her attention back to him.

Pen gave him a sympathetic look. "Detective Prescott told me that they found her body in the park this morning."

"You don't say," he replied, looking shocked. He shook his head in dismay. "I swear this city is getting worse and worse. Lunatics going around killing little old ladies like that."

"I think it was a little more personal than that, and I fully plan on finding out who did it."

CHAPTER ELEVEN

"*He didn't!*"

Penelope's eyes went wide with wonder when she heard those words from Jane as soon as she returned to the office. She hurried in, where she found Benny lazing comfortably in one of the guest chairs with a wicked smile on his face. Jane was at her desk, looking perfectly shocked.

Pen had eaten a bit of lunch before returning, so it was well into the afternoon. She'd also stuffed her small jade-handled gun into her handbag, heeding Richard's warning about the danger involved.

"What wicked stories are you filling my associate's ear with?" Pen queried.

"Just more fabulous tales from last night, a fun little game Cupid devised well after you had departed, sadly. I think you might have enjoyed it."

"Never mind that, we're back to working hours now." She sighed before continuing. "Richard informed me they found Mrs. Abernathy's body in the park this morning."

"Oh no," Jane cried.

Benny sat up straighter. "Well, that was inevitable."

"Benny," Jane protested.

"She's been gone for days. And to leave her dogs like that? My own grand-mère, as she was wont to be called, would have gladly traded in any of her own children before letting anything happen to her little Antoinette—a spoilt little spaniel. Never come between a matron and her pet."

"Now, we know for certain, at least. Richard also told me she still had plans for two on this trip of hers. All the more reason to speak with this dance instructor. Perhaps he was her intended travel companion?"

"Yes, I'm curious to meet anyone who can dance the waltz as easily as the stomp. That reeks of a liberated mind to add to my collection."

"Need I remind you this is a murder case, Benny."

"And I fully plan on being on my best behavior. Besides, I suspect you'll need a man's influence on this case. We can be a wily sort when it comes to love."

Pen gave him a skeptical arch of the brow.

"Don't look at me that way. I've been quite the cad in many a relationship, and have experienced far worse than I ever gave. While he's beguiling you with sweet words and flowery manners, I'll suss out your culprit for you."

Pen pursed her lips to keep from laughing. "Fine, I suppose more heads are better than fewer. Just don't turn this into a farce."

"When it comes to murder? Never, dove."

Pen had called Richard to tell him that Eugene hadn't been certain about Mrs. Abernathy getting into a taxi, just that she had crossed the street. She also gave him a description of the necklace Eugene said she had been wearing when she left.

Jane had called to set up an appointment to view Lachapelle figurines the next morning. Hopefully, Alan Lashbrook would provide enough evidence of guilt, or maybe even confess, such that Penelope wouldn't have to make that tedious trip. Unlike Mrs. Abernathy, she had little interest in the dainty, china figurines. She also had an idea the man who sold them might be the dull, pretentious, blue-nosed sort. However, after being so incorrect about Beau Blackman, she decided to hold off on any pre-judgments.

The Lashbrook Dance Studio was on the Upper East Side, nicely nestled in the kind of neighborhood where one might find lonely, well-heeled matrons looking for a dance partner for the afternoon. Penelope had to congratulate Alan Lashbrook on that bit of contrivance. He was most likely doing brisk business.

It was located on the first floor of a large residential building. A discreet, gold plaque next to a glossy, black door was the only indication as to what the business entailed. Underneath "Lashbrook Dance Studio" written in script was a small addition that read: private lessons.

It gave the appearance of a clandestine meeting or secret rendezvous, that probably tickled his female students in a mostly harmless, but effective way.

"Oh, he is quite shameless, isn't he?" Benny mused, causing Pen to breathe out a laugh.

"I can't imagine he does much business this way. You can hardly see the sign," Jane said, in all her naïve glory.

"That's the point, dove. I just hope we aren't interrupting anything sordid."

"Oh," Jane replied.

Benny pushed one finger into the doorbell, and they all waited. A moment later, a woman answered. She was about as ordinary as could be, homely enough not to cause any envy, but attractive enough to be a presentable face for such an upscale business.

Yes, Alan Lashbrook was quite savvy.

"Can I help you?" The woman eyed Penelope in particular. She scanned and assessed her so quickly Pen would have missed it if she'd been any other woman. She could read instant approval touch the woman's eyes. It disappeared under a curtain of confusion when they landed on Pen's partners, particularly Benny. "If you're inquiring about lessons, Mr. Lashbrook is by referral only."

"Of course, it was Mrs. Dorothy Abernathy who referred me. She has informed me that Mr. Lashbrook is quite versatile."

Now, Pen was the one to study her. If the woman knew of her boss having killed Mrs. Abernathy, it didn't show on her face. Instead, she studied Penelope with even more interest.

"Mrs. Abernathy? Oh, please do come in." She opened the door for them, gesturing to the very tastefully decorated waiting area. It looked more like the parlor of a wealthy household. Alan must have hired a professional because it was fairly modern, but with a touch of that victorian nostalgia that most of his clients probably longed for. The furniture was heavy and overly stuffed, but instead of the dark colors and knickknacks on every surface that Pen remembered from her childhood, it was bright and uncluttered.

"Mr. Lashbrook is with a student right now, but he should be done soon. She is his last appointment of the afternoon, so your timing is perfect. Can I offer you tea or coffee?"

"I'm fine thank you," Pen said. Jane echoed her response.

"Do you have anything stronger?" Benny asked, causing her to blink in confusion.

"He's teasing," Pen said, glaring at him. He pursed his lips and prissily crossed one leg over the other.

"Yes...well," The woman said, returning to her desk, which was a pretty little situation in the corner complete with silk flowers and idyllic paintings behind her that reminded Pen of Beau's work in Mrs. Abernathy's home.

They waited in silence, flipping through the issues of *Vogue* and *Harper's Bazaar* that sat on little tables. Presumably, *Ladies' Home Journal* and *Woman's Home Companion* were too reminiscent of the doldrums of daily life for Mr. Lashbrook's clients. Pen did feel rather elegant sitting there waiting for him to appear.

When Mr. Lashbrook finally did make an entrance, he presented the perfect final touch to the entire picture of the service he offered. He was extremely handsome in a far more refined way than Beau was. His features were better suited to the silver screen than a pirate ship or medieval battlefield, with a dimpled chin, aquiline nose, high brow, and smoldering green eyes.

He was also older than Beau had been, at least in his forties, only barely starting to gray. Considering his profession, it was no surprise to find he had a perfect physique, highlighted by the tailored trousers and dress shirt he wore.

Certainly strong enough to strangle a woman.

"A wonderful session as always, my dear Alan," the older woman with him said in the simpering tone of an adolescent girl. She was probably the same age as Mrs.

Abernathy, but had a very prominent wedding ring on. She also wore an almost gaudy amount of jewelry, certainly real, considering the neighborhood. So he didn't only cater to wealthy widows, but wealthy married women as well.

"It helps to have a partner who dances like a dream," Alan replied, showing off a dazzling smile of perfect teeth as he lifted her hand to kiss the back of it. He waited until she had departed before turning his attention to the three sitting in the waiting area. Like his secretary, he considered Penelope with an appreciative look, his gaze lingering mostly on her fine clothes. His eyes trailed right over Jane, in her more humble attire, as though she were practically invisible. It lingered with curiosity and confusion on Benny, who stared back with an impudent curl of the lip.

"I see we have company, Clarice. Have you been referred to me?"

"Yes, by Mrs. Abernathy," Clarice answered.

His smile froze, and he blinked twice. "Well, that certainly is a surprise."

"Is it?" Pen asked, her brow lifting in mildly innocent curiosity.

He paused, recomposing himself before answering. "My understanding is that she is preparing to leave for distant shores?"

So he knew about her leaving as well, but he gave no indication that he was to be her accompanying guest on those distant shores. Pen decided to reveal the truth.

"She's actually dead. Murdered, it seems."

Clarice gasped in surprise. Alan's face went ashen, his smile disappearing. Pen didn't necessarily attribute that to innocence.

"She was?"

"Her body was found strangled this morning, though it seems she was killed Friday afternoon."

"I...um..." Alan stumbled his way over to an armchair and fell into it. He stared at the floor in concentration, then lifted his eyes to meet Penelope's. "And they confirmed it was her?"

"Yes. She took classes with you on Thursdays, I understand? But not this past Thursday?"

"Yes—I mean, no." He shook his head and his eyes focused on Pen. He sat up, his back rigid. Perhaps it came naturally to him from being a dancer. "I'm sorry, who are you?"

"My name is Penelope Banks, and I'm a private investigator. I was also her neighbor. I'm working with the police on this case."

His gaze narrowed with suspicion. "And why are you talking to me? I had nothing to do with her murder."

"I'm talking to anyone who knew her, which you apparently did. Even her own nephew had no idea she was leaving for an extended trip."

"Well, she hadn't confirmed anything until only recently. She had hinted at perhaps taking me with her, but it never went any further than that."

"So she never directly asked you to go with her?"

"What enjoyment would I have traipsing around Europe as a companion?"

"With a woman as wealthy as Mrs. Abernathy? I can think of many a man who would happily go with her."

"Those men aren't allergic to dogs, which I am. It would have never worked out, traveling with those two dogs of hers. Besides, those men also don't have a thriving business," he snapped.

"Giving private dance lessons to wealthy women, one on one?"

"Yes, and there's nothing wrong with that," he said, quirking an eyebrow defensively.

"I noted that she had quite the array of music selection in her home. You teach modern dance as well as the classics?"

"You young people today," he said in a scathing tone. "You seem to be under the impression that all people over a certain age are perfectly set in their ways, incapable of appreciating anything new and modern. You'd be surprised. Yes, Dorothy was just as much a fan of the Charleston and the Foxtrot as she was the Waltz and Pasodoble."

"Of course, I didn't mean to imply otherwise. Did you only meet on Thursdays?"

"Yes."

"No other days?"

Alan's gaze narrowed with suspicion. "We were social acquaintances," he said cautiously.

"What exactly does that mean?"

"Exactly what it sounds like," he snapped. "I'd take her to dinner, dancing, the ballet, things like that."

"She's asking if your companionship extended into the bedroom, my good man," Benny asked in a bored tone.

"I beg your pardon?" Alan was red-faced with outrage. Pen noted how hard Clarice worked to keep a straight face behind him.

"My...*assistant*," Pen glared at Benny, who pressed his hand to his chest with mock offense, "was being rather careless with his language. But I do have to ask whether or not you and Mrs. Abernathy—"

"That is none of your business!"

"The police would ask you the same question, perhaps

even taking you to the station to do so. It would be much easier for you to—"

"I think you should leave now. I have no interest in answering any further questions from a *private* investigator. I don't care if you are working with the police. In fact, I have serious doubts about that. Let them come and question me if they like."

"If they do, they certainly won't be kind enough to wait until you have no clients. How would they feel seeing a police car parked right outside your studio, and several officers lingering, interrupting a private lesson to ask you about one of your dead clients—your murdered client? You know how quickly rumors spread among ladies like those to whom you give lessons."

Alan stared back in horror, no doubt imagining that scenario.

Pen continued in a more congenial tone. "One of the benefits of being a *private* investigator is that I have a more delicate touch. I will be very considerate of your clients and their privacy, as well as yours. As far as anyone looking outside their windows is concerned, we're just three interested prospects for your lessons. I can't say as much should my detective friend barge in."

He narrowed his eyes, seething at her, but he didn't insist that she leave. "No, my relationship with Mrs. Abernathy was not...what your friend was so salaciously insinuating. I simply escorted her to functions. We had a shared love of music and dancing, something her husband never allowed her."

"Did she ever mention a Beau Blackman?"

There was a flicker of recognition on his face before he smoothly extinguished it. "The name is familiar. I believe he painted a few pictures for her," he said indifferently.

"Not exactly high art, but what one appreciates in a museum is not always what one would like to see on their own walls, I suppose."

Pen's eyes flicked to the walls of the waiting room that displayed a similar sort of art as that found in Mrs. Abernathy's apartment. "Of course."

Alan gave her a cynical smile. "The same rule applies to my place of business."

"Of course," she repeated. "Do you know if Mrs. Abernathy was also a social acquaintance with someone who works at either Aristotle Book Dealer, or a shop that sells Lachapelle figurines?"

"I do know she frequented both establishments quite regularly. I wasn't a particular fan of the figurines, but I wasn't about to be dismissive of her interest in them. As for that book dealer, well...he certainly made a mint off her, taking in all those first editions and in return selling her books that were good for nothing but pulp if you ask me. But she loved her shocking little cheap yellowback books, didn't she?"

That certainly gave Penelope an idea of where to take her investigation next. Perhaps Mrs. Abernathy was catching on that her book dealer was underpricing what her books were worth?

"Just one final question, where were you Friday afternoon?"

He looked defiant for one moment, then sighed heavily. "Friday afternoon, I will have to check my appointment schedule."

Clarice spoke up. "I can look—"

"I don't always go through Clarice to book appointments, especially Friday afternoons. There are some clients who prefer lessons in the privacy of their own homes."

"It was only four days ago, surely you remember where you were?"

"I had a number of errands to run as well. As for my clients, short of a subpoena or warrant or...whatever, I don't intend to give up their privacy for this tawdry business."

"Even if it means clearing you of suspicion?" Pen asked in disbelief.

"*That* is just how much I value their privacy," he said in a lofty tone. He rose from his chair, hinting at a dismissal.

Pen shook her head in wonder. "You realize the police are going to insist on an answer."

"All I can claim is that I was running errands. I don't have a foolproof alibi for Friday, that hardly means I killed Dorothy. She was...a very special woman, and I shall miss her dearly."

He sounded sincere, but Penelope couldn't get past how vague and inconsistent he was about where he had been Friday afternoon. It was obvious he didn't have an alibi, at least one he'd be willing to give up so easily.

As it was, she had no more questions so she rose as well. Jane did the same almost immediately, but Benny was deliberately leisurely about it. He gave Alan a look that had him shifting uncomfortably. That wasn't anything unusual. Benny liked to make everyone uncomfortable. Just one of the many ways he fought his seemingly constant boredom.

Once outside, Penelope sighed. "So, what do we think?"

"He sure seemed awfully guilty toward the end. He didn't even give a proper alibi. Most people know what they were doing this past Friday," Jane said.

"And he pretty much confessed to something more than a simple professional relationship with Mrs. Abernathy," Pen added.

"He was very handsome," Jane acknowledged.

Benny began laughing. "Oh you two, it's really quite adorable how you've both missed the obvious."

"And what is that?" Pen asked, feeling her irritation set in. She recalled how perfectly disruptive he'd been during her questioning.

"Alan Lashbrook is—how shall I put it?—a member of the same fraternity as yours truly."

Pen blinked in surprise. Jane, to her credit, caught on almost instantly and her jaw dropped. "But he—all his students are women, aren't they?"

"And quite wealthy. Money is a great motivator, dove."

"How can you even be sure?" Pen gave him a skeptical look.

"Trust me. Why do you think I was so pointed with my questions? In fact, I'd say that might explain where he was on Friday. There are certain clubs for men, who are so inclined, to gather and commiserate like sad little pansies." He smirked as though there was a cryptic meaning there. "If you stop looking at me like a child who's misbehaved, perhaps I'll introduce you to the group I'm thinking of, which does in fact have a social meeting Friday afternoons?"

Pen blinked in surprise, then smirked. "Well Benny, it seems you've earned your keep after all."

"Does this mean I get to keep working with you?" There was something in his expression, beneath all that insouciance and smug demeanor, that hinted at eagerness. Pen could relate. There was something quite satisfying about a good and honest day's work, especially for such a rewarding endeavor.

"I suppose so. For now, let's go back to the office to review everything we've learned and see if Richard has had more success than we have."

CHAPTER TWELVE

J ane was busy writing all the information they had gathered about Beau Blackman and Alan Lashbrook on her beloved chalkboard. In the meantime, Pen was trying to learn more about Benny's astonishing assessment of the latter.

"So this club, dare I ask how you know about it?"

He gave her a droll look, not bothering to answer.

"Yes, I know, you're...similarly inclined. But you said it was for older gentlemen."

"And thus insufferably genteel. Don't worry, it isn't like anything you've heard about bathhouses and other places."

"Bathhouses?" Jane's stick of chalk stopped mid-word and she turned to Benny with a look on her face that indicated she wasn't sure she wanted to know more.

"They're like health centers, with pools and such," Pen said, hoping that would satisfy her enough. It was obvious Jane didn't fully believe it, but she left it alone.

Benny chuckled. "If you're going to deal with murder cases, you certainly need to know more about the unsavory underbelly of New York, dove."

"Jane's experienced quite a bit over the past year. She's no lamb," Pen said proudly, causing Jane to turn to her with a pleased smile.

"Yes, yes, well, aren't we supposed to be learning more from our dashing detective?" Benny hinted.

"Yes!" Pen said, happy to have a reason to call Richard.

Once she was finally connected, he didn't sound hopeful. "It's been a series of dead ends so far. It took some time to get in touch with the maid and the cook. Mrs. Abernathy apparently let them go early on Friday, just before she left for the day. Both had solid alibis for the afternoon.

"As for information, her maid, Sally, wasn't very fruitful. Mrs. Abernathy was a perfectly adequate employer, not a tyrant, but not indulgent either. I sensed some bit of disapproval with how, and I quote, 'frivolously some women could live their lives.'"

"Did she indicate whether Mrs. Abernathy ever had gentlemen company in her home for, say, personal reasons?" Pen couldn't help but recall what Beau Blackman in particular had hinted at.

"Not that they told me, though they might not have said out of loyalty. I didn't sense any animus, particularly since they were left with glowing references and parting gifts of a nice sum, though Sally declined to say how much it was.

"As for her cook, Martha, well, she was quite a fountain of information. She seemed suspiciously skittish at first, but that's because I learned she had been given permission to clean out the kitchen stores, everything up to and including the dogs' food."

"She stole the dogs' food? And that wasn't suspicious?"

"She claims the lady of the house gave her permission to take it all. Still, she swears she left the dog food, as she had no use for it. She told me that Mrs. Abernathy was moving in with someone during the weeks leading up to her travel overseas. She doesn't know who. She had planned to take the dogs with her, of course."

Pen considered that. "That means a moving company. I'll check through her things for any contracts she may have had set up."

"If you find out let me know."

"Of course."

"And was your day any more enlightening than mine was?"

Penelope told him about their visit to the Lashbrook Dance Studio, including Benny's assessment of Mr. Lashbrook.

"And he's certain of that?"

"If anyone would know, it would be Benny. It's probably best if I am the one to visit this club rather than the police, don't you think? You'll just scare them into silence."

"You may have a point. But don't mistake mannerisms for meekness. We could be dealing with a murderer, or at least someone covering for one."

"Yes, detective," Pen said with a smirk. "I assume the jewelry search wasn't successful?"

"Obviously. That would have been too easy. I suspect our killer is holding onto them until the case dies down or he's found someone to work with outside of our known circles. Granted, even if those known circles weren't exactly heralded for their willingness to tell the truth, they mostly trade in small-time goods, snatched gold chains, and pick-pocketed watches. The kind of jewelry Mrs. Abernathy was wearing would probably scare most of them off."

"I have a few known circles myself, ones who might be far more willing to converse with me than a member of the New York Police Department."

"I can't ask that much of you, Penelope."

"Then don't, I'm offering it. Besides, I'm rather in the mood for a drink, anyway."

"I'll pretend I didn't hear that."

Pen laughed. "Yes, detective."

After ending the call, Benny turned to her with a grin. "Did I hear something about a drink?"

"How do you feel about a night at the Peacock Club?"

"You had me at Peacock, dove."

CHAPTER THIRTEEN

Penelope was surprised at how insistent Jane had been on coming along with Benny and her to the Peacock Club. Pen wasn't so much worried about what her fiancé Alfred would say—he wasn't the sort to dictate how she lived her life—it was that she was such a duckling when it came to drinking.

Being regulars, and friends of Lulu, who performed there, they were granted immediate access and escorted to a table in the VIP section of the club. Lulu wasn't performing that night, but she was there, enjoying herself as always.

"I'm glad you're here, Lulu," Jane said, with glittering eyes.

"Me?" Lulu asked, giving her a skeptical look. Even after several adventures together, they weren't nearly as close as Pen was with either of them separately. She suspected Jane was still slightly in awe of the woman.

"Yes, I wanted to give you this." Jane reached into her large handbag and ceremoniously handed over an envelope with elegant script on the outside. Jane turned to Benny, giving him one as well. "And this is for you."

Benny and Lulu both glanced at one another, then down at the envelopes. They opened them and pulled out a thick card, also with elegant script.

"You're inviting me to your wedding?" Lulu asked in surprise. She lifted her gaze and offered Jane a half-cocked smile, looking skeptical.

"You three are the closest I have to friends in this city. I know you think I'm perhaps not as worldly or smart and a little meek and timid, but—"

"You stop that right now," Lulu said, reaching across the table to place a hand on Jane's which were fiddling with nervousness. "You are smart, and more importantly loyal. As for being worldly, Pen told me about you saving her life that time. How many people would shoot a man like that?"

Jane colored violently. "That was mostly—"

"A brave and wonderful thing, and I would be honored to go to your wedding, Jane. But...are you sure you want that? Pen has told me a thing or two about your folks and—"

"And nothing," Jane insisted. "It's time they learned that I'm not that same girl from Poughkeepsie, that I have a wide variety of friends and an amazing job and a wonderful fiancé despite their constant complaints about him." She glared into the distance and Pen had an even better idea of how the past weekend had gone for her. "I'm a new Jane Pugley."

"Soon to be Jane Paisley," Pen said, lifting her glass of champagne in salute.

"Thank God for that," Benny said, also lifting his glass. "And don't worry, dove, I shall do everything in my power to make a spectacle, such that your parents write you off for good!"

Jane laughed, and didn't object when he poured her a

glass of champagne, to which she was notoriously susceptible. "I suppose this does call for a glass of bubbly," she said.

They all lifted their glasses in celebration, and then sipped.

"Now then," Lulu said, quirking an eyebrow at Pen. "I know y'all didn't come all the way up here to the Peacock Club on a Monday night just to deliver a wedding invitation. What is it you're really after?"

"It's my neighbor. She was found dead this morning."

"Oh, well that's a terrible thing," Lulu acknowledged. She tilted her head with curiosity. "Still, there's a long distance between your 5th Avenue apartment and Harlem, honey."

"But there may not be between the jewels that were stolen from her and a certain someone here who might know a few people who would be more than happy to pay for those jewels."

"I assume you're talking about Tommy?"

"Obviously."

Tommy Callahan was, by then, the official right-hand man of Mr. Jack Sweeney, one of the more notorious gangsters in New York City. He traded in everything from illegal gambling to illegal booze and all things in between. He owned the Peacock Club, which was how Pen knew both men. She had once made a living by playing cards there, using that strange mind of hers to mostly win.

Lulu chuckled and shook her head. "Boy did you pick a bad night to ask a favor of him."

Pen frowned and looked around the club. "Where is Tommy? I thought he conducted most of his business from here."

"He's here every night," Lulu said with a small scowl

and twist of the lips. "Tonight there's been...a minor distur-
bance, let's just say."

As though on cue, Pen saw Tommy storm from one of
the back rooms. He had in tow a blonde girl who couldn't
have been more than seventeen, wearing a fringed red dress.
He was practically dragging her across the dance floor,
which magically gave him and his stowage a wide berth.
She looked about as happy as a wet cat, and her claws were
certainly out, ready to scratch his eyes out. However, it
seemed her mouth was doing all the damage, giving him a
good acidic mouthful, if the looks on both their faces were
any indication.

"She sure doesn't look happy," Jane said.

"Happy? That kitty cat is ready to attack," Benny
observed.

"I recognize that red dress she had on. She was here last
year."

Lulu turned to give Pen a look of awe, which quickly
cooled into a knowing smirk. "That brain of yours. You
must have some witch in you."

"I got enough of that kind of talk from my father
growing up, thank you," Pen said with a frown.

"That was a compliment," Lulu said with a laugh.

"Still, I've never seen Tommy put up with something
like that from anyone, not even you Lulu."

"Because I know better. Tommy needs to be handled a
certain way."

"Is that his younger sister?" They both had blond hair,
though the girl's was more of a strawberry blonde compared
to his, which was almost white.

Lulu breathed out a laugh. "You could say she's family.
Just don't ask him about it when he's finally cooled down
enough for you to ask a favor."

"Perhaps I shouldn't tonight."

"Nonsense, you're one woman he'd like owing him a favor."

"I'm not working for Mr. Sweeney, especially now that I don't have to."

"And yet, here you are up here with all us sinners," Lulu said with a sly look.

Pen pursed her lips. Lulu had a point. It wouldn't be the first time she'd come up to this part of town seeking information. Heaven knew she was no saint either. Perhaps in her career it was a good idea to keep one foot firmly planted in the wicked underworld. It seemed a benefit, even for cases that involved wealthy widows from 5th Avenue.

Tommy stormed back into the club, sans angry little girl. Even from her perch, she could see those jade irises of his brewing up a storm, daring anyone to cross him. That was odd. Usually, Tommy kept a level head no matter what. She'd seen him face down a gun and not so much as blink.

"Go on, now is probably the best time to ask him a favor. He'd relish forgetting about that little problem he just took care of."

Pen gave Lulu an uncertain look, but decided to trust her judgment. She'd been the one to steer her towards playing cards when she barely had two nickels to her name, and that had turned out far more optimistically than she could have hoped.

With that reassurance, Pen rose from the chair and purposefully walked toward the back where Tommy had disappeared. The area was guarded by one of his goons, who weighed at least twice as much as she did. He recognized her, but that didn't prevent him from putting one hand up to stop her.

"I need to speak to Tommy."

"You sure you want to do that tonight? He ain't in a good mood."

"Perhaps I can change that," she said with a smile.

The look he gave her indicated exactly how he interpreted that, and she felt her face warm.

"I need a favor from him," she explained, realizing too late how that didn't help anything.

He laughed softly and gestured for her to proceed. Rather than argue to save her virtue, she went in.

Tommy was at a table to himself, smoking a cigarette as usual and staring at the drink in front of him. His handsome face was still taut with tension. His long lean body, in his trademark white suit, seemed one second away from snapping in two.

"Well, well, well, to what do I owe a personal audience with Pen Banks?" Tommy said without looking up. Pen was encouraged by the hint of humor in his tone. He did so enjoy taunting her.

"I need a favor."

That got his full attention, those green eyes sliding up to meet hers with icy curiosity. "You got a lot of nerve asking for favors after what you pulled just before Christmas."

"How do you know that was me?"

The look of disdain he gave her told her it was a stupid question. Of course that little casualty from her last case would be traced to her.

"Does that mean I shouldn't bother asking for help?"

He chuckled. "Call me curious."

"I suppose I should get right to it then. Do you know anyone who would be able to buy stolen high-end jewelry, the kind that might be worth ten thousand or more?"

He smiled, though nothing about it was amicable, and

leaned back in his chair to consider her. "Funny you should ask."

Pen blinked in surprise. She hadn't even described Mrs. Abernathy's necklace yet. "Have you heard something?"

"About your little lost ring or whatnot? No. But I happen to have done some recent business with a few folks who handle that sort of thing. What is it you're looking for?"

"A necklace," Pen described it from what she remembered.

"Anything with that many stones might eventually find its way to people like them. Unless whoever stole it decided to cut them." He gave her a considering look. "Did they kill whoever they stole them from? If so, cutting them would be the smart thing to do."

Pen felt her disappointment set in. She thought about Beau and Alan. Both were cunning in their own way, certainly savvy enough to realize how recognizable a necklace like that would be.

"Don't look so down. You'd be surprised how stupid most crooks are," he said with a laugh. "I'll ask around about your little necklace, Pen."

"I'd appreciate that," she said cautiously.

"I'm sure Mr. Sweeney would enjoy you owing him a favor for once."

"I'm not going to work for him, if that's what he plans on asking from me in return."

Tommy chuckled. "Yes, Pen, I believe he received that message loud and clear. Still, one of these days he may come knocking for a favor in return. It would be in your interest to answer the door."

Pen almost reconsidered. Mr. Sweeney surely knew that she was involved with a detective. He wouldn't be dumb enough to ask her to do something illegal, at least not *terribly* illegal. He had plenty of men like Tommy to do things like that for him. More likely, he'd want her to do something only someone of her stature could accomplish—or someone with her strange ability to remember things. That, she could handle.

She thought of poor Mrs. Abernathy, her body lying there under a pile of snow after being strangled—maybe even with her own necklace, which had then been unceremoniously stolen from her. She deserved better than that. The least Pen could do was find out who had killed and robbed her.

"You have a deal."

CHAPTER FOURTEEN

P en made it home late, but not too late to take Dot and Dash out for their final walk of the day. Alice had come by earlier to see to them, but after so many hours inside, they were restless once again.

"Would you prefer I see to the dogs?" her butler asked.

"You're too good to me, Chives," Pen said with a sigh. "But no, I can't ask that of you. Besides, a walk in the brisk air will give me time to think."

In retrospect, she wasn't happy about how her adventure at the Peacock Club had gone. Owing a favor to Mr. Sweeney wasn't something anyone wanted on their shoulders. Still, looking down at Dot and Dash as she led them to the service elevator, she thought it was the least she could do for their former mistress. After all, whoever had killed her had almost left them to die as well.

With that renewed determination filling her veins, Penelope felt slightly invigorated as she led them out onto the sidewalk. Even this late at night, there were people strolling about, and the streets were well-lit enough that she didn't feel any danger.

However, crossing over into the park was a different story. The 69th Street entrance had enough lighting, but beyond the pathways, the darkness loomed in that part of the park where it was nothing but nature. Still, she felt safe enough, especially with two large dogs.

While Dot and Dash sniffed around for a place to finally relieve themselves, she considered everything she'd learned that day.

Mrs. Abernathy was going away for a year and taking one of her suitors with her. Beau had confessed to being one of those suitors. If Benny was correct about Alan, he was more of a friend than a lover. Pen could see how either, in their own way, would be desirable as a travel companion. But it seemed neither of them was her intended guest.

So, was it the book dealer or whoever sold her the Lachapelle figurines? Perhaps someone else?

The sound of Dot and Dash growling drew Penelope's attention. She looked down to find them both alert, looking out into the darkness beyond the path.

"What is it, girls?" Pen asked, feeling her trepidation set in. She strained to hear the sound of a shoe crunching into the ground, or a branch snapping. It was difficult to tell with the sound of the dogs and the noise of the city beyond the park. "Alright, let's go back."

Before she could tug them out of their defensive stance, one of them barked. The next moment, Pen had the wind knocked out of her. She fell back into the frozen grass, the human canon ball falling right on top of her. She was too shocked to even scream at first. Fortunately, Dot and Dash made enough of a ruckus for her, barking and growling.

"Help!" Pen finally managed to get out before he clamped his hand over her mouth. Panic began to set in as he held her down with his heavy body and his other hand began to wander. She writhed and wriggled underneath him, hoping to avoid whatever he had planned. Then she stopped, surprised when she realized he was trying to wrest the ends of the dogs' leashes from her hand.

Before he could free them, he let out a loud yelp and a curse as one of the dogs bit his thigh. He rolled off of her to get away from them, but now both dogs had the scent of blood and lunged for him. He should have been grateful Pen had clung to the leashes, as that was the only thing that stopped them from going after him.

He ran, barely even limping, though his hand was pressed against his right thigh as though in pain. Good, thought Pen. She hoped it hurt and became infected. It was an uncharitable thought, but some men didn't deserve any better.

She took a moment to recover, realizing she was still shaking over the incident. In all her adventures, even in the days when she'd played cards in some very questionable places, she'd never been attacked like that.

Dash and Dot, went quiet and came back to her, sniffing and nosing her coat as though to comfort her. She smiled and reached up her free hand to pet them.

"Good girls," she murmured, hearing a slight tremor in her voice. She got up on shaky legs and led them back to the park exit. Her eyes darted back and forth waiting for the man to come back and have another go at her. She didn't bother with the service entrance to the building, instead rushing right in through the front doors. That late at night, she hopefully wouldn't have to worry about other residents having to share the elevator.

"Good evening Miss Banks," Stephen, the night

doorman greeted. "I see you've taken on Dot and Dash. It's a terrible thing that's happened to Mrs. Abernathy, and just across the street from us."

"Yes, it is," she said, realizing she might have also suffered the same fate if not for Dash and Dot. She quickly wished him a good night and rushed to the elevators hoping she wouldn't become hysterical before getting to the eleventh floor.

Chives, God bless him, was still up and waiting for her out of professional duty. The moment he saw her, he knew something was wrong.

"What happened, Miss Banks?" He relieved her of the leashes and she fell onto the bench in the foyer, taking a few deep breaths.

"Someone attacked me in the park."

He gave a look of alarm which she dismissed with a wave of the hand and a weary smile. "I'm fine, thanks to Dot there. Dash did her part too. Nothing more than a good knocking over and a bit of a scare. He certainly came out the worse for it. You go and see to them, while I pour myself a bit of gin."

"I think it would be wise to contact the police."

Pen nodded. At the very least she suspected the attack was related to Mrs. Abernathy's murder. Still, the last thing she wanted right now was a bunch of uniformed men and hard-nosed detectives barraging her with questions.

When she finally got to her feet, she was grateful to be so personally close to a member of the department. So she called him directly.

Richard answered after a few rings, having been caught already asleep.

"Richard?"

"Penelope, what is it?" he asked, instantly alert.

"I...I..." Suddenly it was too much to even repeat what had happened. Thankfully, she didn't need to.

"I'll be right there."

CHAPTER FIFTEEN

By the time Richard got to Penelope's apartment, she was in a much better state, which was good. As much as she marveled at the heroic way he instantly flew to be by her side without her having to utter more than a word, she didn't want to play the wilting violet just to garner sympathy. The gin had helped.

Cousin Cordelia, who had woken up during all the commotion, most certainly hadn't.

"Really, it was nothing. As I stated, I was simply knocked down. I even landed in a patch still covered in a bit of snow. I barely have a bruise really."

"It was most certainly not nothing!" Cousin Cordelia argued, looking at Penelope as though she had gone perfectly insane. "Oh, to think what would have happened if Dot and Dash hadn't been there! You might have suffered the exact same fate as poor Mrs. Abernathy."

That thought certainly hadn't been lost on Penelope. She had been attacked in the same area where her neighbor had lost her life, perhaps to the very same man. She felt her legs get shaky and she cautiously settled on the couch in the living room.

"Thank you, Mrs. Davies," Richard said. "I should question Penelope in private, this being an official police matter at this point. It would help her give a more precise account if there are no distractions."

It was the "official" that won her over. "Oh yes, of course. The very idea, mad men attacking decent people, and in this part of the city! Is no one safe anywhere?"

"All the more reason for me to catch him," he hinted.

"Well, I shall be safely in my room. I don't think I'll ever leave after all of this!"

When she disappeared, Penelope exhaled, giving Richard a grateful smile. "Thank you for that."

"Of course, but I was being truthful. You gave me a brief summary of what happened, but knowing you, I'm sure there are more details you can give now that we're alone."

"Almost alone," Pen said, noting that the two dogs were with them in the room. They also seemed too worked up to go to sleep. It didn't help that Little Monster had decided to occupy one of their beds. She'd deal with him later, as they seemed happy sniffing around at the new arrival.

That made her think of something. "I think they knew him, my attacker. They sensed him hidden in the trees and began growling, as though suspecting something was about to happen."

"Perhaps they just had a bit of premonition. Dogs can be uncanny that way."

"Perhaps. Either way, they knew right away the man was questionable for some reason."

"Obviously a good reason."

"He was going after the leashes, which was odd."

"Which only confirms that it must be related to Mrs. Abernathy's murder."

"When his hand first started wandering I thought for certain he was about to…" Penelope swallowed hard, not stating her thoughts aloud.

Richard's jaw hardened and his dark eyes gleamed with anger. Noticing how shaky she became, he silently took her glass and quickly poured another finger of gin for her. Once back on the couch next to her, she felt comforted by his strong presence. She fell into his side, allowing herself to be delicate and vulnerable for once, despite herself. She had probably earned it that night.

"I'm fine, it's just still so—"

Richard put his arm around her, pulling her in closer. "Don't be embarrassed or apologetic, Penelope. This is a normal reaction. I've seen men twice your size and ten times as stubborn overcome by similar experiences."

"You actually know someone more stubborn than me?" Pen said with a soft laugh before taking a sip.

Richard smiled. "Just tell me what else you remember, whenever you're ready."

She nodded. "I wish I had more to tell you. Honestly, it happened so quickly. I couldn't even pick him out of a lineup. He was wearing a hat and a scarf over his face. I couldn't see his eyes, it was so dark. He was strong, and taller than me. So far that fits both Beau Blackman and Alan Lashbrook from what I saw of them today." She paused. "I just wonder why he'd be going after the dogs?"

"Perhaps it's what you said, that they knew him."

"Yes, but why would that matter? I assume all the men she…associated with had at least visited her in her apartment. Perhaps their last interaction wasn't so pleasant, hence the growl in warning."

"That might make them useful for identification purposes, something I wouldn't have thought to do. Your attacker may have inadvertently played his hand."

"Especially with the souvenir Dot left him," Pen said with a bitter smile of satisfaction.

"From now on, I'm going with you when you walk them this late at night. No arguing, Penelope."

"I wasn't going to. Though, I do feel bad about it. You coming all this way just to help me walk them across the street for a while."

"I don't object to the company," he said with a grin.

"I always welcome seeing you as well." She looked down at Dot, now resting at her feet. "Perhaps I should take them along with me tomorrow, see which man they growl at."

"I should ask you to step away from the case but, as you just admitted, you're too stubborn for that."

"I am, and I already have a vested interest."

"What does that mean?"

"Do you really want to know?"

"I most certainly do now," he said pulling away and turning to stare at her.

"I don't like us having secrets between each other so I'm going to tell you and trust that you understand I know what I'm doing."

"That doesn't give me much reassurance."

"I may owe Jack Sweeney a favor."

"What? *Penelope!*"

"I told Tommy I wouldn't do anything illegal for him."

"Oh well, if you promised that then all's well."

"Being sarcastic doesn't suit you, Richard."

"How about angry? Honestly, I probably shouldn't even know this information as it tiptoes dangerously close to aiding and abetting some crime, I'm sure of it. There's no reason for you to put yourself at risk that way."

"Except for one poor widow who was murdered right outside my front door. You said you hadn't had success with the necklace, the very thing that could solve this case. I used what resources I had. Besides, as you well know, it isn't the first time I've worked with him, all for the greater good I might add."

Richard stared at her a moment longer, then sighed and fell back against the couch. "What's done is done, and yes, I do hope you know what you're doing, Penelope. I'll just claim an anonymous tip came in if, by some stroke of luck, you do manage to solve the case with that connection."

"Who knows? Perhaps tomorrow's adventures with Benny's connection will save us the trouble."

"I think perhaps I should accompany—"

"Absolutely not. You know where we're going. None of those men Benny discussed will talk to a police detective. Even with the book dealer and at the shop for Lachapelle, it will be far easier to coax information from them without your badge interfering."

"I suppose," he grumbled.

"Besides, I have my little gun and now I know how to use it. I wish I'd brought it out with me tonight. We might have solved the case that much quicker, and avenged Mrs. Abernathy's death."

"Don't go killing anyone if you don't have to Pen, it's... something that can haunt you."

Pen turned to Richard, whose eyes focused hard on the wall ahead of them. He didn't talk much about his experience in the Great War, other than to tell her how he'd first volunteered early on, and how he'd gotten the scar. Still, he must have killed at least a few men during his time serving.

"Perhaps I'll be like Dot, only I'll aim a little higher and get him right in his *gluteus maximus*," she said with determination.

A smile broke out on Richard's face, then a laugh escaped his lips. He pulled her in closer again. "This is why I always enjoy our arguments. You never cease to delight, my dear, even when I want nothing more than to leave you handcuffed to your bed for your own good."

"Richard," Pen scolded in a teasing manner, "not in front of the dogs, you'll make them blush."

He coughed out another laugh and squeezed her shoulders. "Yes, it seems they are quite the protective sort. It may be a good idea to take them along with you, after all."

CHAPTER SIXTEEN

A s much as Penelope would have liked Richard to spend the night, she knew Cousin Cordelia might have made a fuss about it come morning. She was still quite old-fashioned. Pen didn't mind, as it made their trysts all the more exciting. Instead, she'd rescued Dash's dog bed from the claim of Little Monster and carried him to bed with her. She pitied the man who tried to attack her while he was there by her side.

Pen made sure she woke up early enough to meet Alice when she came by for the dogs' first walk of the day. She wanted to warn her about what had happened the night before, and go with her when she took the dogs out. Surely, Pen's attacker wouldn't make another attempt when he had two people to contend with, to say nothing of the dogs.

At five minutes past eight, she began to worry. The day before, Alice had been there precisely at the top of the hour. Pen had no idea how prompt she usually was about time, but considering the circumstances, she was inclined to assume the worst had happened. Being perfectly restless, she stopped pacing and decided to go down and check for her approach.

When she opened the door, she was surprised to see Alice in the hallway further down, and even more surprised to see who was there with her. Alice was in tears, no doubt because a perfectly uncomfortable-looking Walter Abernathy had just imparted the news about his aunt.

"Oh, Alice," Pen said, rushing down to her. "I see you've heard about poor Mrs. Abernathy."

"I, um, I'm afraid I hadn't realized she hadn't been given the news. I just assumed since she had been working with you and the detective that she would have heard," Walter said, looking as though he wished he could go back in time to the moment he had let it slip, in probably the clumsiest manner if his expression was any indication.

Penelope wrapped an arm around Alice, whose face was buried in a handkerchief. Pen noted it had the initials A.W. on it. "It isn't your fault, of course. I meant to tell Alice when she arrived today. We only just found out yesterday, after all. I suppose as next of kin, you were the one the police contacted?"

"Yes. I...I wish I could take back all the things I said regarding her. If I'd known..."

"It's just so terrible. Who would do such an awful thing?" Alice cried.

"Come, let's go inside. I'm sure the dogs will be happy to see you." And hopefully cheer her up, Penelope thought. She turned back to Walter as they walked. "Did you come to see me as well?"

"I, er, no, I was told to come here and make note of anything that might be missing from among my aunt's things. I'm not sure why they think I might know anything, as I rarely visited her."

That brought about a fresh round of tears from Alice, and Walter closed his eyes in self-reproach, probably wishing he could take back those words as well.

"Before you do that, perhaps you could come and sit with us for a moment. As you know, I've been investigating this case and I've discovered a few things. You may have some valuable insight to offer."

His eyes fell on Alice in her arms, and he instantly nodded. "Of course."

Pen eyed him, watching to see if there was any hitch in his step. On the surface, it seemed his only hindrance in walking was the foot he had already put in his mouth. That, and the way he stumbled over himself when it came to Alice. Still, she wasn't going to discount him as a suspect so quickly. She knew by now that family members were always likely candidates when it came to murder.

The three of them went to the living room. Penelope and Alice sat on the couch while Walter took an armchair across from them, his focus was entirely on Alice. He didn't hesitate or wince while contorting his body, or when the backs of his thighs met the cushion. More importantly, Dot and Dash did nothing more than sniff at him curiously, then quickly return to greet their favorite person in the world, tails wagging as they crowded Alice, seeking her attention. Pen had been doubtful of him as her attacker, but it was nice to have it confirmed.

"Again, I must apologize for stating the news so bluntly."

"No," Alice said, shaking her head and sniffing one last time. She brought her eyes up to meet his. Even her red eyes and tear-streaked face couldn't dim how pretty she was. "As you stated, I had no idea, though I should have been prepared for such awful news. I should be the one apologizing for my reaction."

"No, you were much closer to her than I was, her own nephew," he said frowning as he stared at the floor. "I dismissed Aunt Dorothy as somewhat frivolous, when in reality she'd always been nicer to me than even my own parents. Certainly more than Uncle Spencer. Still, I'm glad she reached out last year, encouraging me to join her for the holidays. If I'd known..."

"Don't beat yourself up over it, Mr. Abernathy," Alice said kindly. "She did say how she admired the way you turned out."

"Is that so?" he asked swallowing with embarrassment. "As I stated, I was asked to have a look around Aunt Dorothy's apartment to see if anything was missing or unusual. I decided to come before I went to work. Granted, you probably know more about the usual state of it than I do, Miss Winterfort."

"Please call me Alice."

Walter blinked and swallowed hard, his wondrous eyes staring at her with his restrained version of delight. As though Penelope needed any more proof that he was quite dizzy for the girl.

"And, er, please call me Walter." He hesitated, his face coloring a bit before he continued. "Perhaps you'd like to accompany me? You're probably more familiar with it than I am."

"Yes, of course," Alice said shyly. She lowered her face to the dogs. "But first these two need their walk."

"Before you go, that's one other thing I wanted to talk to you about. It's good you're here as well, Walter." She turned back to Alice, who gave her an inquiring look. "Last night while walking Dot and Dash, I was attacked by a man."

Pen held her hands up at the instant expressions of shock and sympathy that came from Alice and Walter.

"I'm fine, don't worry. Still, it was obvious that he was after the dogs for some reason. I can't fathom why, can you?" She addressed that specifically to Alice, who would know best.

Alice shrugged, her face still masked with concern. "I mean, they're lovely dogs, but to go to all that trouble for them is a bit much."

"It seemed like they recognized the attacker, could that be it?"

"Well, these two are usually pretty friendly around strangers, but they also make good guard dogs. If they'd met him before and didn't like him, or if he'd posed some kind of threat to Mrs. Abernathy then that might explain it."

"So, it could be related to her murder then," Pen confirmed. "All the same, Alice, I should go with you this morning in case he makes another attempt."

"Nonsense, I'll be just fine, it's daylight already."

"Perhaps I should go instead?"

Alice and Walter had both spoken at the same time and turned to each other in embarrassed amusement.

"I was thinking perhaps it would be more reassuring for you to have a man by your side, no offense to Miss Banks, of course."

"None taken," Pen said with a wry smile.

"That's very kind of you Mr. Ab—"

"Walter, please."

"Walter, but as I stated, it's daylight. There were already people in the park on my way here. Besides, these two seem to have done a fine job as far as protection."

"They did get a good bite in last night," Pen said with a small laugh. "But Walter is right, I do think you should go with him at least for today. Unless you think perhaps another man you're seeing would object?"

Alice colored violently. "No, there is no other man—I mean *any* man. I'm not seeing anyone at the moment."

Walter exhaled ever so slightly, and Pen smiled with satisfaction.

"Well, then, I'm sure we can trust Walter to be a gentleman?" She turned to him with an inquiring look.

Poor Walter blinked, as though she were asking seriously. He sat up straighter with indignation. "Of course, I would never lay a finger on Miss Winter—"

"Alice,"

"On you, Alice," he said addressing her. "I also do a bit of boxing, if that offers you more reassurance."

"You do?" Alice said, for the first time staring at him with interest, perhaps even a bit of girlish intrigue. It never failed.

"That must be why you fill out your suit so admirably," Pen said with a pert smile, enjoying how uncomfortable he became under the compliment.

"We should, um, probably get going," Alice said, distractedly pressing a hand to her cheek which looked rather warm.

"Yes, yes, off you two go," Pen said, rising from the couch and shooing them in encouragement. "But be very aware of anyone lurking nearby. I'm sure those two darlings with you will once again step in to save the day. Or perhaps you could throw a good punch for me, Walter?"

"I...suppose," he said, uncertain whether she was joking or not.

They went on their merry way, taking Dot and Dash with them. Pen breathed a sigh of relief. Although she had offered, she hadn't relished the idea of putting on winter wear to accompany Alice with the dogs. Truth be told, she was still quite shaken from last night and hesitant to go back to the park so soon. She was glad she would have Richard to accompany her that night.

Pen waited for them, if only to make sure their trek was without peril. The walk lasted much longer than Alice's had the day before. When the two of them returned, they both looked like rosy-cheeked cherubs, each with bright glittering eyes.

"So, did anything happen while you were out?"

Both their eyes grew wide, and they inadvertently stepped away from one another. Perhaps it was simply a matter of being back in the warm apartment, but a bit more blood crept back into their cheeks. Pen smiled and held back a laugh.

"It was...pleasant," Alice sat cautiously.

"Yes, quite pleasant," Walter eagerly agreed, as though that was something safe enough for both of them.

"Well, bully for pleasant walks," Pen teased.

"I've agreed to accompany Miss—Alice again this evening. Just to make sure she's safe of course," he quickly added.

"Thank you," Alice said, turning to him with a neutral expression, though her eyes glittered.

"Yes," he said looking back and simply staring for a moment. He remembered Pen was there and turned back to her, clearing his throat. "I plan on looking through Aunt Dorothy's apartment this evening, as I really should be getting to work."

"Of course," Pen said.

He cast one more lingering look toward Alice, who was, for once, timid and speechless. Then, he quickly left.

"How fortunate to have him with you for your walks, just in case anything should happen while you're out."

"Nothing did happen," she said defensively, interpreting Pen's words in entirely the wrong way. She lowered her eyelashes. "I mean, no one was attacked."

For shame, Pen mused, deliberately interpreting those words in entirely the wrong way. She wondered if Walter had the gumption to be such a passionate lover. Still, he was playing the hero, and he was handsome enough, which would hopefully lead to something more fruitful.

"I should really be getting to work as well," Alice said, suddenly eager to leave. She fell to her knees and nuzzled Dot and Dash one final time before handing them over, making her goodbyes, and fleeing.

"What do you gals think, can we make something of those two?" She wanted to think their tails wagged a bit more fervently at her question, but perhaps that was wishful thinking. Still, Dot did manage one bark, followed closely by Dash.

"Yes, I agree."

CHAPTER SEVENTEEN

"What are those?" Benny stared down at Dot and Dash as Penelope led them into her office later that morning.

"Oh, aren't they just darling?" Jane said, rushing from her desk to bend over and greet them.

"How did you arrive before me?" Pen stared at Benny in shock. "A second day in a row waking up before ten in the morning? Surely a scientific journal needs to be written about this strange phenomenon. Or perhaps Folger's should discover your secret and somehow add it to their cans of coffee."

"As if I'd miss out on one second of this little investigation of yours." He grimaced down at the Dalmatians, who simply quirked their heads back at him with curiosity. "I hadn't realized there would be guests of the four-legged variety working with us."

"They're here for a reason. I was attacked last night and they protected me." Once again she indulged the reactions of sympathy and surprise for just a moment before continuing. "They didn't seem to like the attacker very much. I think, if they were to run into him again, they'd have the same reaction. Fortunately, they left him with a nice incriminating souvenir just below his derriere."

Jane tittered and Benny smirked. "You mean we get to force men to remove their trousers? I really need to consider taking up a career in private investigation." That caused Jane to giggle even more.

Pen pursed her lips at him. "I doubt we'll be allowed to get that far. But since we're indulging in low humor, I believe you were to take me to a certain gentleman's club."

"At this obscene hour? And you accuse me of being low. No, no, Pen, that meeting can only be held once the sun at least passes midday. We must begin with your book tradesman or that shop which deals in figurines. I vote for the latter, I'd like to see what all the ballyhoo is about."

"Well, our appointment isn't until eleven. I suppose we can go by the art school first and see if our nude model has a nasty dog bite this morning. Now, that we have an idea when Mrs. Abernathy was murdered, I'd also like to find out exactly where he was Friday afternoon."

"And my day just became that much brighter. Oh Pen, you really must invite me along on more of these escapades of yours," Benny said with a clap.

He made sure to stay well behind Jane as Penelope led the way back out, the dogs ahead of her. She had procured the services of Leonard once again, knowing she was far less likely to get a taxi to stop for her with the dogs in tow.

"I can see it's going to be a crowd," he said with a good-natured grin. "Like something from a circus."

"Well, I intend on sitting well away from the ring with the dog tricks, thank you. I'll sit up front with you, my good man," Benny said.

"And yet they seem to like you so much," Pen teased. "Usually dogs are a good judge of character."

Benny gave her a dry look before opening the front passenger door for himself. In the back, Jane got in first through the door Leonard held open for her. Pen urged Dot and Dash inside, then got in behind them. As spacious as the car was, it was rather a wild ride with two excitable dogs in back with them.

"I fear we won't be allowed to take them into the gallery and school. Leonard needs to stay with the car, and I don't want to leave them cooped up inside."

"I'll watch them," Jane eagerly offered, which was exactly what Pen hoped for. Benny, of course, would never pass up the chance to see the impressive Mr. Blackman again, and Pen needed to do the interrogating.

"Thank you, Jane," Pen said, then led Benny inside.

At the art school, she once again inquired at the front about Beau.

"He's teaching today, taking over landscapes for Mr. Marcus until we can find a replacement, but that class should be ending soon if you don't mind waiting again."

"Well, phooey," Benny said in a droll voice as they passed the time looking at artwork in the hallways. "You don't suppose he teaches in the same clothes he models with, do you?"

"You're perfectly shameless, Benny."

"Always, dove."

They eventually saw students exiting into the hallway. They made their way to the room in which Beau was teaching. Much to Benny's disappointment, he was dressed that morning. His long hair was loose around his shoulders. As un-modern as it was, Pen had to admit it was extremely appealing. She wondered how many men reconsidered the current fashion of trim cuts plastered to their skulls with pomade after seeing him.

The same female student lingered behind to chat with him. Penelope and Benny waited just inside the door for them to finish their discussion, though it looked more like a bit of flirting considering the smile on the girl's face. It went on long enough for Pen to wonder if the student was deliberately holding Beau up just to make them wait.

Finally, Beau made a point of turning to acknowledge them with an amused expression. "Portia, it seems my interrogators are back once again to question me. Miss Banks, how can I be of service today?"

Portia glared at them, Penelope in particular. She wasn't a pretty girl, her eyes were a bit too close together and her nose was too snubbed. However, Penelope could sniff out wealth even from a distance. The art classes were probably her way of being idly rich until it was time to marry.

Pen brought her attention back to Beau. He'd been standing in the same place since they entered, so it was impossible to tell if he was suffering from a dog bite. "I think perhaps we should speak in private. I have some rather unfortunate news about Dorothy Abernathy."

Beau's smile faded. "She's dead isn't she?"

"Yes, I'm afraid so. Murdered, in fact. She was strangled."

Portia gasped in horror. Pen hoped that might be enough to get her to leave, but instead, she reached out to cling to Beau's arm in sympathy. He patted her hand distractedly and focused on Pen again.

"When did it happen?"

"That's actually why I'm back. If you could tell me where you were Friday, it would avoid the police having to come here and ask you."

"I'm afraid I can't answer that."

Pen blinked in surprise. "You do realize the police will ask you the same question."

"And I'll have to say the same thing. I know it makes me look guilty, but I didn't kill Dorothy. I had no reason to."

"She was wearing a necklace worth thousands of dollars. That would be enough to give anyone a reason."

Beau's brow furrowed, as though concerned about this new possible motive. Portia sniffed, as though she didn't consider that much of a reason. He placed a quieting hand over hers.

"All the same, I didn't kill her and I certainly didn't steal any necklace of hers. I am sorry she's gone."

"Could we sit for a moment? I'm rather weary." Pen said, studying him harder. She hadn't written him off yet, mostly because he had yet to even take a step.

He gestured to the stools around the classroom. "Please, but I'm not sure what else I can tell you."

Pen took a seat and Benny sat on a stool next to her. Beau remained standing in place, as did Portia.

"Is there any part of Friday from, let's say, late morning until that evening that you can tell me about?"

"If you must know, he was with me that afternoon," Portia finally said in a huff.

"Portia," Beau said, only half-heartedly.

"No, if you're going to go to prison for something you didn't do, I won't stand by and allow it. I know you'll get in trouble with the school, but surely this is an extenuating circumstance?"

Beau sighed, considered her for a moment, then turned back to Penelope. "Yes, I was with Portia that afternoon. I have a private, unofficial seminar with a handful of students

Friday mornings, then I had lunch with Portia and...well, we spent the afternoon together."

"In a hotel, if you must know," she said almost proudly, giving Pen a smug look.

"I see," she said, still not quite ready to dismiss him as a suspect. Portia was a little too smitten to be a reliable alibi. Still, If that was true, he most likely didn't kill Mrs. Abernathy. But that didn't completely absolve him of other possible crimes. "And last night, can you tell me where you were and with whom?"

His brow wrinkled in confusion. "Home alone, I'm afraid. What happened?"

"A related crime, though I'm not at liberty to divulge the details."

"Then I suppose I should expect a visit from the police, though I've done nothing wrong."

"And you were quite *close* with Mrs. Abernathy." Pen studied Portia to see if she had any reaction to that. The way her eyes rolled told her that she knew everything. "They'll want to confirm his whereabouts on Friday, which means you'll probably be questioned as well, miss."

The smug smile came back. "And I have nothing to hide. This is a modern age, Miss Banks. Young women don't need to be imprisoned in the home only to be married off as cattle anymore."

Just how old did she think Penelope was? Rather than get offended, she found it amusing. "Well, I'm sure the police will be pleased with how much of yourself you're willing to expose to them."

Portia narrowed her eyes with contempt.

"Speaking of exposure..." Benny hinted, sounding impatient.

Pen gave him a constrained look of exasperation, then

turned back to Beau. "Forgive my friend, he's a bit of an aficionado of human anatomy. Are you planning any more modeling sessions this week?"

Beau gave a self-effacing laugh, bowing his head with humility. "I was helping a fellow art teacher after a model failed to show up."

"Beau is quite generous in that way, always helping other teachers. One day he'll be the top teacher here. I, myself, have already spoken to—"

"I'm sure they didn't come here to learn about my career as an art teacher. I'm truly saddened by Dorothy's death, but as you can see I wasn't the one to kill her."

"You can check with the Barlowe Hotel," Portia said. "We were in a suite and had several deliveries of room service throughout the afternoon...and evening. We had worked up quite the appetite, you see."

"I most certainly do." Much more than she would have liked. If anything, Portia was far too accommodating.

Penelope would leave questioning the hotel to the police. She was familiar with the swanky hotel, and a place like that wouldn't be giving any information without a warrant or subpoena.

But he still hadn't moved from where he was standing, and he didn't have an alibi for last night. Pen didn't want to dismiss the idea that there could be two different culprits in the whole affair, or perhaps even two working together as coconspirators.

"I suppose that's all for now. Thank you for giving us a moment of your time," Pen said, rising from her stool. She stumbled and fell in the direction of Beau. He and Portia simply stared at her as though she was a lunatic when she landed face-first on the floor.

"Are you alright?" Beau asked, leaning over with a look

of concern on his face. Portia clung to his arm even then, bending over as well, though she looked less worried about Pen's welfare.

"I'm fine, just clumsy, I suppose," Pen gritted out as she came to her feet. She supposed with Portia draped over him as though she were glued on, it would have been difficult for him to react in a way that any gentleman would, leaping to her defense. Not that Beau was necessarily a gentleman.

He had leaned over without a wince, but that movement wouldn't have necessarily caused a dog bite to flame up in pain. His status as her attacker was still in limbo.

She turned to see Benny giving her an utterly droll look, as though he knew perfectly well she had stumbled on purpose and was quite amused it hadn't gone as planned. She scowled at him and walked toward the door. He chuckled and slowly caught up to her.

"That went well," he teased in a whisper.

"No thanks to you. You could have at least offered to help me," she hissed back.

"You should have told me you were going to play the damsel in distress, dove. Like you, I was waiting for Sir Galahad to step in and rescue you."

"I'd like to see how you would have gotten him to expose the fact that he might have a bite mark on his thigh."

Benny stopped suddenly, just before they had reached the door. Pen watched as he turned to address the other two. "Mr. Blackman?"

Beau and Portia stopped the furtive and animated discussion they were having, and looked his way.

"I'm thinking of hosting an impromptu artist salon sometime this week. I was quite impressed with your, ah, physique. I would be willing to hire you to serve as a model for a few hours, you name the fee."

Up until the mention of money, Beau had given Benny a wary look as though he wasn't sure it was the kind of event he'd be interested in.

"Any amount?" Beau asked skeptically, a crooked grin on his face. "How about one thousand dollars?"

"You drive a hard bargain, but...done!"

Beau blinked in surprise. Portia gaped, looking appalled.

"But, I will need a brief preview, for my own reassurance you see."

"You want me to take my clothes off? Now?"

"I'd be willing to offer a minor advance of, say, one hundred dollars for your trouble."

"He most certainly will not!" Portia scoffed.

"I'm afraid Portia does have a point. I don't think the school would look too kindly at me getting naked outside of a class session. I'd hate to be accused of being a degenerate," he said with a knowing smirk.

If there was any suggestion in that remark, it rolled right off Benny's back. He was used to subtle barbs of that nature.

"Suddenly so shy?" Penelope mused. "A lot of men, and women, would jump at the chance for such an amount. I would, and I've never even posed nude before." At least not in America, Pen reminded herself. She had gone through her own period of degeneracy in Spain just before her father had cut her off, perhaps rightfully so.

"You don't strike me as the type who needs the money, Miss Banks," Beau said wryly. She couldn't fault him for that barb.

Portia glared at them, clinging to Beau even more firmly. "You two give those of us with money a bad name, dangling it in front of people in the hopes that they'll jump to any of your demands. It's despicable. But Beau has self-worth and too much pride to stoop to groveling like that. I think you should leave now."

Pen did feel rather abashed at Benny's shameless offer. Yes, it had been far more straightforward than her attempt, but there was something to be said for frankness.

"We're sorry if any offense has been taken. It was a clumsy attempt to see if Mr. Blackman has any bite marks on his right thigh. A young woman close to this case was attacked last night and may have been murdered if not for one of her dogs coming to her rescue. It would be a simple matter of Mr. Blackman showing us his upper leg to eliminate him as a suspect." Pen had deliberately addressed Portia, just in case she wanted to reconsider the alibi she was providing for Friday. She might learn the truth soon enough during any upcoming trysts in hotels.

"Which only makes it that much more insulting," Portia said instead. "I've already told you Beau had nothing to do with what happened on Friday, he was with me. Why would he try and kill someone last night?"

Beau was perfectly content to stay silent, allowing her to do the talking, and Pen couldn't blame him. It probably would have taken a warrant just to get his pants down, if only for the insult Portia was piling on to any injury his pride may have suffered. He'd look like a fool if he lowered his trousers at that point.

"Again, thank you for your time," Pen said, taking Benny by the arm and leading him out.

"I tried," he said breezily.

"You most certainly did," she retorted. "And we're no closer to knowing if he attacked me or not."

"Do you believe the alibi for Friday?"

"I don't know. She's obviously dizzy for him, with the kind of adoration that might provide a false alibi. She seems like the type that the police wouldn't give more than a slap on the wrist if she was lying, and she probably knows it. Still, with a date and location that's easy enough to confirm, she may have been telling the truth. Our Mr. Blackman moves on quickly."

"Looking like that, he should. The man is a perfect adonis, why not use it to take advantage of rich women?"

"All the more reason he wouldn't have to steal jewelry to get by. Thus, we're off to our first interview of the day. Let's peruse the Lachapelle shop and see if we can't find our murderer."

CHAPTER EIGHTEEN

The shop that sold Lachapelle was as quaint and whimsical as anyone would have imagined. It might as well have been lifted right from Rue Cler in Paris. The name Lachapelle was stretched above the windows in gold lettering, which was all the advertisement it presumably needed. There was a hint of Art Nouveau flair to the decor surrounding the sign, though not enough to seem too bohemian.

Through the paned glass on either side of the French doors, shelves and tables were lined with small, china figurines dancing, embracing, wooing, contemplating, and, daringly enough, even kissing.

Jane was once again in charge of Dot and Dash, much to her delight, despite the weather. She'd naturally have to stay outside, but Pen had a plan to bring the proprietor to the front door. She could see him through the windows of the door, already with a look of disapproval on his face as he eyed the Dalmatians.

The sign in the window reminded any visitors that the shop was open "by appointment" only. Pen knocked on it, giving him a questioning look. He frowned and walked over to open it for her.

"Are you Mr. Percy Dawson?" Jane had given Pen the name of the owner after making the appointment.

"I am, and I'm afraid the dogs are to remain firmly outside. I shouldn't even have to say it."

Dot and Dash paid him no attention whatsoever. They were too absorbed with the idea of potentially going on another walk.

So, he hadn't been her attacker from last night it seemed. Still, that didn't mean he couldn't be Mrs. Abernathy's murderer.

Pen studied him. He looked to be in his forties, handsome in an imperious sort of way, with a pinched nose, sharp eyes, and a mouth that seemed inclined to turn down at the sides. Beneath his very well-tailored suit, he was sturdy enough to have the strength to strangle a woman.

"Oh, of course, I just wanted to make sure I was dealing with the owner. You are the gentleman Dorothy Abernathy always personally dealt with, I assume?"

Any hint of disapproval on his face quickly vanished, replaced by an intense study of Penelope, with just a hint of suspicion. He was probably surprised she was an acquaintance of someone old enough to be her mother. "I am. Do you know her?"

"Yes, she recommended you to me."

"She did?" Again, his surprise was understandable. His typical clientele was either much older or probably quite a bit younger than Penelope. That duality where one was so easily enthralled by the idea of love, or simply nostalgic for a different period.

"Yes, and I'm quite interested to learn more," she said truthfully.

An overly obliging smile came to his face. "Mrs. Abernathy was a dear and valued customer."

"Was?"

He blinked quickly, his smile fading. "Well, she had intimated to me that she would be going abroad for some time." He forced a smile again. "Naturally, when she returns, I hope she will resume her relationship with our humble shop. Do come in."

Pen gave a subtle glance to Benny as they entered past the door Mr. Dawson held open for them. He seemed to have also picked up on how quickly Percy had recovered from his blunder.

"And she didn't offer to take you with her?" Pen asked in a teasing way. Really she hoped his reaction would reveal that he too had been asked, or had wanted to go but was denied.

"Well, I couldn't very well leave this shop now, could I? I'm the only one who can run it as it should be run," he said, just as teasingly.

Though, Pen did notice that he was the only one there. Most shops had at least some boy or girl to lend a hand with minor chores like stocking wares or keeping track of receipts. Perhaps that was a benefit of being by appointment only.

"May I ask how it is you know Mrs. Abernathy?"

"I'm her neighbor. I had admired the figurines in her home and she told me this is where she'd bought them."

A smug smile curled his lips, and he briefly lowered his eyelids in acknowledgment. "Yes, this is the only shop in New York, on the entire East Coast, really, where one can procure an authentic Lachapelle." His mouth turned down slightly. "There has recently been a new store opening in Chicago."

"She must have been an admirer, she had so many of them."

"Oh yes, Mrs. Abernathy was a bona fide collector. She, of course, saw the value in owning such magnificent pieces. It's an investment, really. Each design is created in lots of one hundred—that's worldwide, mind you. We obtain a single piece for display purposes, and only remove it once the entire lot has run out," he said, guiding them around the store as he casually gestured to one piece or another.

"Though, beyond just their monetary value, Mrs. Abernathy appreciated the sentiment behind the Lachapelle ethos. The pieces are meant to call upon a more genteel time, a period where romance and courtship were imbued with a degree of gravitas. There used to be a day when it truly meant something simply to kiss a woman. Today, you can find young, unmarried men and women getting on in the most sordid ways everywhere you look, with no heed to propriety or decency."

"Shameful," Pen said with overt disapproval.

When Mr. Dawson turned away, Benny elbowed her in the side and silently laughed.

"Now then, are you interested in starting your own collection of Lachapelles? It is never too early to get started. Some of the pieces you see here only have one left in their lot. They may be gone by tomorrow."

He was a decent salesman, Pen would give him that much. If she had any interest in the twee little things, she might have been tempted to buy. Looking around, there were quite a few on the shelves still. Even she knew he should have spread them a bit thinner, if only to give each piece its own importance, as any high-end luxury shop would. In its current state, the store looked more like a shop of cheap curios, specializing in one particular item.

"Did Mrs. Abernathy have an appointment with you this past Friday?"

"Friday? No, she had a standing appointment to come on Mondays."

"Are you open Fridays in the afternoon?"

"By appointment, yes. Is that when you would like to set up a regular viewing? I do try to work with clients on their schedules, even occasionally making house calls...for the right customer." There was a subtle jab Pen sensed in that qualifier.

Penelope decided to be perfectly frank with him. She had a feeling he was inclined the same way that Benny and Alan Lashbrook were, which would have made him another of Mrs. Abernathy's acquaintances and nothing more.

"I should confess that I'm more than Mrs. Abernathy's neighbor, I'm a private investigator. I'm sorry to have to tell you that Mrs. Abernathy was murdered Friday afternoon."

Mr. Dawson's face fell in shock, an expected reaction. Certainly a reaction that anyone could manufacture in an instant. "Murdered?"

"Yes, did she ever indicate to you that she was worried about anyone? Had anyone made threats against her?"

Percy seemed to be still absorbing the news of her murder.

"Mr. Dawson?"

"Yes," he said, blinking and focusing once again.

"Yes, someone had made threats against her?" Pen asked in surprise.

"No, at least not that I know of. I meant, yes, Mrs. Abernathy did consider me a confidant of sorts. We were close, very close. I'd accompany her to museums, and join her for dinners out. She never intimated to me that she felt she was in danger. This is...very troubling."

He wandered to the counter, his hand coming to his forehead.

"Did she perhaps want a more...personal relationship with you?" If anything, his disdain or embarrassment might confirm what she already expected.

Instead, his gaze narrowed on her. "What does that have to do with anything?"

"There are indications she was killed by someone she knew, someone she felt comfortable with."

"And you suspect me?"

"I'm only helping the police eliminate suspects. If you have an alibi for Friday, I'd be happy to pass it along. I'm sure you'd rather that than having some uniformed officers stomping through your front doors and bustling around in your shop, perhaps while you are with a valued customer?"

"As it happens I was with a private customer on Friday. I certainly won't be giving the name, only for them to be imposed upon by some flat-footed policeman. If a *detective* would like to question me, they too can make an appointment. Seeing as how there couldn't possibly be a shred of evidence against me, they have no reason to act as the literal bull in a china shop by intruding upon my working hours. Now, if *you* would so kindly leave the premises."

Benny and Penelope left without further comment. When Percy ceremoniously shut the door on them, she turned to give him a look.

"I take it he's a member of your fraternity?"

"One would think, but no."

"Really? Are you sure?"

"One never really knows, but the signs were off. Though, I suspect his interest in Mrs. Abernathy was purely mercantile."

"Yes, I suspect the trade in Lachapelle is waning. He has no help in the store. I know once upon a time women liked to collect little items like that to fill their cupboards. Today, not so much. If he really only displays those pieces that have some left in their lot, that's quite a few to choose from."

"It was rather cluttered. No wonder he was so heart-broken to learn of her death. He seems to need all the business he can get."

"He didn't really give an alibi for Friday. Still, Dot and Dash didn't react to him, so I don't think he was last night's attacker.

"Handsome all the same though. Your Mrs. Abernathy certainly liked her men a certain way. And they were apparently social with one another."

"Don't speak ill of the dead, Benny."

"Who's speaking ill? I truly admire the woman. I wish I had that much vigor."

"At any rate, he may have had motive. If she was leaving for a year, she couldn't shop here. Perhaps he tried to plead with her to buy a few more before she left. Then, upon seeing that diamond necklace she wore he decided to get his payday another way?"

"You're the expert when it comes to murder, dove."

Pen gave him a wry look. "Let's at least visit this book dealer before making any conclusions. He may have guilt written all over him, no pun intended."

CHAPTER NINETEEN

When Jane returned from walking Dot and Dash, they all crowded back into the car. Penelope related everything that had happened in the Lachapelle shop.

"Do you suspect he's in danger of going out of business?" Jane asked, her head leaning around the dogs, who were amazingly enough not yet tired.

"I don't know if things are that dire quite yet, but business doesn't seem to be booming."

"On the other hand, diamonds never lose favor," Benny said.

Leonard chuckled. "You know, the funny thing about those little figurines, Miss Sterling used to laugh at how so many of her friends were addicted to buying them." He shook his head in wonder.

"Don't tell me Agnes collected them too?" Pen asked in surprise.

Leonard laughed. "Oh no, she had far more taste than that. Smarts too. No offense, if you like them, of course."

"Not particularly."

"I think they're rather lovely," Jane protested.

"Of course, they're darling," Pen reassured her. "Leonard didn't mean anything by that."

"Not at all, Miss Pugley," Leonard said, secretly catching Pen's eye with a conspiratorial look. "And you certainly aren't alone in admiring them. They were so popular there was big business in trading them. I heard one rare piece was going for something almost a thousand bits of kale."

"A thousand dollars?" All three of the car's other human occupants exclaimed at once.

"There's a black market for everything it seems," Pen said in wonder.

"I'm not even lying. Miss Sterling told me it was similar to some tulip thing that happened in Europe somewhere."

"Yes, in the seventeenth century when they became highly in demand."

"Yeah well, both equally head-scratching if you ask me. In a few months, this city will have tulips sprouting up everywhere. Just plant them. How rare can they be?"

"Rarity can be manufactured. I'm pretty sure that's the business model of Lachapelle. They only create each figurine in lots of one hundred."

"Yeah well, that's the thing. They were so popular, suddenly you had some enterprising crook deciding he would make his own imitations. By all accounts, they were pretty decent replicas, even down to the stamp at the bottom. Apparently, the real thing uses some kind of additive in their glazing process that easily distinguished them." Benny laughed. "I can just picture a hundred pearl necklaces all being clutched at once when the New York matrons realized they had paid a small fortune for a fake back then."

Pen was surprised she hadn't heard about it. Granted at the time she didn't read the papers as often as she did now. She thought back to Benny's party when the bullfighter had mentioned his grannie had decided to stop buying them a few years earlier. That must have been when the fakes had been discovered.

"I'm sure no one admitted to having fallen for a fake," Pen said.

"You'd better believe it. Miss Sterling and me, we had a good chuckle over how many of them suddenly disappeared from the parlors of mansions all over New York."

While it was never a nice thing when someone was chiseled in that manner, Pen couldn't bite back the smile of amusement that it had been over something so frivolous. Then again, weren't tulips equally frivolous?

Human nature was a strange thing.

She briefly wondered if that might have had something to do with Mrs. Abernathy's murder. It happened a few years ago. Still, she had been collecting them for some time now, despite that. It would have been awfully coincidental for her to point the finger just as she was leaving the country.

They had arrived at the Aristotle Book Dealer shop. They followed the same routine of Benny, Jane, and Penelope exiting the car with Dot and Dash in tow—or rather, leading the way.

That shop was open for business to anyone who wanted to walk right in, but the inside was such a jumbled mess of bookshelves and cases, Penelope didn't identify anyone that she could call to the front door to see if Dot and Dash would react.

"Let me have the leashes," Pen said, reaching out to Jane.

"Are you sure? I don't think the owner would be happy about them going inside."

"That's what I'm counting on," she said with a wink.

Benny grinned as he opened the door and held it for her. There was a bell above that alerted the proprietor that he had customers. It also gave Dot and Dash enough of a jolt to bark a few times.

"What the—are those *dogs*?" A man came from around a bookcase, he reeled back as soon as he saw the dogs and Penelope. She couldn't tell if it was fear or incredulity. Whatever it was, he lost his footing and tripped over the edge of a bookcase, falling back and yelling in surprise. Dot and Dash joined in, barking at the commotion.

"Take those dogs out right now!" He shouted as they continued to bark. He cursed and struggled to get to his feet, hissing in pain as he tried to step on his right foot.

"I'm so sorry," Pen apologized. She hadn't expected such a reaction—unless it was an act.

"Well, now I've probably twisted it," he protested, trying to step on it and wincing.

Penelope handed the leashes to Jane to take them outside. While she did that, Pen studied the owner as he leaned against a bookshelf to give his ankle relief. He was as handsome as the others, quite dapper, in a professorial way. He wore a tweed coat, wool vest, and trousers. His full head of hair was sprinkled with enough gray to give him a mature look, though his face was contorted with outrage.

"How dare you bring dogs in here. Have you any idea how valuable some of the volumes in here are?"

Her ruse had been futile. She couldn't tell if the dogs

were reacting to a man they'd once seen before and didn't particularly like, or in response to his verbal assault and fall.

"What in heaven's name would compel you to bring two dogs into an establishment that deals with rare books?"

"I apologize, I hadn't realized how rare your collections were. I simply saw the shop and couldn't help but enter. I'm Penelope Banks and this is Benny. We're very interested in buying and selling, Mr...?"

"Comeau, Taylor Comeau." He exhaled and tugged at his coat and vest, straightening them. "Was there something in particular you were interested in?"

"Do you deal in only rare and valuable or would I be able to obtain dime novel books here as well, Mr. Comeau?"

He looked at her as though she had suggested using his most valuable edition to prop open a door. "I can obtain almost anything for the *right* client."

"And what makes one the right client?"

He considered Penelope and Benny. A quick scan over their clothes, and she sensed his instant approval. "Do you have any books you wish to trade or sell? Perhaps any first editions? Books with limited runs?"

"Quite possibly. Does a first edition of *Call of the Wild* appeal to you?"

It was quick, but Pen noted how the color in his face paled a bit while his eyes lit up

He quickly recovered. "Yes, I do believe I could find one or two buyers for that."

"Would I be able to obtain a few books by Belinda Cartwright, say, as a trade?" It was the name printed in some flowery script on the spine of a few cheap books in Mrs. Abernathy's library.

He blanched, but his eyes sparkled with delight. "I

believe I would be able to trade that in for say...four or five books of hers?"

"Wonderful!" Pen said with empty-headed glee. She turned to Benny, who couldn't help the sardonic look on his face. "I knew Mrs. Abernathy wouldn't have steered me wrong."

"Er, Mrs. Abernathy?"

Pen turned to find him giving her a more considering look. "Yes, she mentioned she had done business with you, trading in her late husband's books for those she was more interested in owning."

"Yes, I of course have done quite a bit of business with her. When exactly did she mention my shop to you?"

"It has been some time. Has she been in recently? When did *you* last see her?"

"Oh, recently," he said ambiguously, before quickly moving on. "Now as to Belinda Cartwright, that might take me some time to procure. In the meantime, why don't you bring your volume by and I can give you a thorough assessment as to its value. Do you have any other such volumes? I'm willing to make house calls, if needed."

"Quite a few. But let's start with that one. How much do you think I could get for it?" Penelope stared at him like a doe in the woods.

"It's impossible to say without inspecting it myself. There are so many things that go into a valuation, I wouldn't want to get your hopes up beforehand. The market is so fickle."

Penelope knew a swindler when she saw one, and Mr. Comeau was a perfect example. The vague language, uncertain promises, and patronizing address, it did nothing to lessen her suspicion.

"I do know she's going away for some time. My father—

he owns a financial firm on Wall Street—has asked about the remainder of her late husband's collection. Was she leaving that with you to handle? He'd be very interested in buying the whole lot, if so."

It was as though he could see the kale growing right before his eyes. "Naturally, she would go through me, as always. I could certainly obtain those volumes and sell them at a reduced combined purchase price."

"You could?" Pen said with overt glee. "Oh, he'd be ever so grateful, and with his birthday only a few weeks away! So she's agreed to have you handle selling them?"

He paused before continuing. "Of course, it's still in the negotiation phase."

"Of course. Not that I would know anything about such things," Pen said, hoping she sounded dim enough to fool him.

"Don't say anything to your father just yet. I'd rather he be happily surprised at what I can do for him, rather than disappointed should things fall through."

"Oh yes, of course."

He was lying through his teeth. Pen suspected there was no such deal in place. Perhaps he didn't realize Mrs. Abernathy was dead, and he hoped to plead his case to her. Or perhaps he planned on breaking in to get them. Maybe he had his own key?

"Now then Mr. Comeau," Pen continued, leaning in with a pert, conspiratorial smile. "I hear she was traveling abroad with a plus one. She didn't confide in you who that might be, did she?"

His jaw tightened ever so slightly before he loosened it with a smile. "I'm afraid I wasn't quite that much of a confidant to Mrs. Abernathy. I can only speak to her literary interests, I'm afraid."

"Oh," Pen said pulling back. "And I thought for sure one of mother's friends said she had seen her with a man at a museum, or perhaps having dinner at a restaurant. Now that I think on it, he certainly matches your description."

Taylor swallowed hard. "Yes, Mrs. Abernathy and I were social...on occasion. I was very fond of her and she of me. It was more of a convenience for both of us. You see, I'm a widower myself. I opened this shop after my beloved wife died," he said, looking around with a moony smile. He sighed contentedly, then brought his attention back to Penelope. "It was pleasant enough to spend time with Mrs. Abernathy. However, I could never leave my beloved shop for so long." Again he looked around as though falling under the spell of the dusty books around him.

No, Taylor Comeau was in love with that shop more than anything. He wouldn't have been tempted by the offer of a year-long trip to Europe. "So you have no idea who she was going with?"

"Well..she did tell me she was waiting to hear back from someone before she made any final plans—I assume that was with whom she was traveling."

"But she didn't give you a name?"

His eyes narrowed with mild disdain. "I'm not in the business of gossip, Miss Banks."

"Of course," Pen said, tempering her irritation and plastering a look of self-admonishment on her face. "Well, I'll be in touch about the books."

"Yes, please do," he said, instantly changing his tone as though realizing he may have lost a customer.

"Good day, Mr. Comeau."

He made sure to remind Penelope to come back as soon as possible about her book, insisting she take a business card from him before she left.

"Not *entirely* disappointing. Frankly, as abysmally as this case is going, I learned more from him than anyone." She gave Benny a dry look. "Can I safely assume he is only interested in women?"

"Frankly, I think that dull man would marry his books before he'd become involved with any person, man or woman."

Pen laughed. "Yes, even Mrs. Abernathy would have seen that much. So he wasn't a candidate for this trip of hers. He'd never leave this bookstore behind. I'm guessing it was his late wife's money that paid for it."

"Perhaps he killed her as well."

Pen considered it for a moment, then shrugged. "Too much of a coincidence. Though, I won't completely dismiss the idea. I do know he's certainly not an honest business-man, swindling women who probably don't know any better out of their rightful value."

"Still a diamond necklace is a diamond necklace. Maybe theft was the motive for murder. How many books could it have bought him?"

"That's a good point. Another interesting observation was his reaction to Dot and Dash. If he was close to Mrs. Abernathy, surely he would have known what breed she owned? How many Dalmatian duets do you see around Manhattan?"

"They certainly had a reaction to him. Do you think he's the one who attacked you last night? That stumble was quite the act, don't you think?"

"Yes, I had considered he was faking it. Sadly, all these men have a similar enough build. You were right about her having a certain type, even if he is older than all the other possible candidates. Still, he's not so old he couldn't tackle me to the ground."

"Should I go back inside and ask him to take his pants off?"

Penelope laughed. "No, but I do think it's about time we checked up on Mr. Lashbrook with this social club of yours."

CHAPTER TWENTY

P enelope decided they should all eat lunch back at her apartment. Cousin Cordelia was more than happy to join them. Pen knew she simply wanted the details of the case, particularly one so scandalous in her view.

"*Four* men? All of whom she...socialized with? My goodness. At least when poor dear, Harold died, I had the decency to remain faithful."

"I don't see anything wrong with moving on after one's husband dies. I should think he'd want you to find love again. Just look at Jane and Alfie and how happy they are."

"Jane has gone about it in a proper fashion. Mrs. Abernathy..." Cousin Cordelia couldn't finish, looking aggrieved and all but performing the sign of the cross.

"I say, the more the merrier. Why not take advantage while one is still able?"

"Benny, you're a man; of course you would say such things. If society didn't keep you young men reined in, you'd galavant around with a different woman every day of the week—women of a certain ilk, mind you."

Benny caught Penelope's eye across the table and gave her a wry look. Even Jane next to him smiled to herself.

"You'll be happy to know that I have never been that sort of womanizing cad, my dear Cordelia. In fact, I'm taking Penelope to visit a group of men such as myself who positively *abhor* the idea of galavanting around with women of easy virtue."

"Oh, how delightful. It's so reassuring to know that society hasn't completely gone to the wolves."

"At any rate," Pen said, giving the highly amused Benny a censuring look. "We're going to find out if one of our suspects was, er, patronizing this men's club when Mrs. Abernathy was murdered. At the very least that will narrow down the suspects."

"Perhaps you can tell me the details, thus far. I may be of help. After all, while I may not have been as... promiscuous as our neighbor, we do both come from the same generation. Having seen her apartment, I'd even go so far as to say we have *some* similar tastes and interests."

It wasn't a terrible idea, and Penelope often found that relating the facts aloud loosened some nugget of a clue for her. She told Cousin Cordelia about each visit with the four suspects, and what they had claimed.

"She was going to take a man half her age—one who's perfectly content posing nude—with her to Europe?" Cousin Cordelia asked, scandalized. "Well, I imagine the *Europeans* don't take issue with such a thing, particularly the French. Still, it's quite disgraceful."

"I still don't understand why he would pass up the opportunity," Benny said. "All he would have to do is be a companion on a first-class trip around Europe."

"Perhaps he was tired of being a...*companion*." Pen said. "Besides, he has the besotted *Portia* to cater to his needs now, she's younger and conveniently adoring. Also, according to Taylor Comeau, Mrs. Abernathy found a replacement companion."

"But who is it?" Jane asked.

Pen considered it. "So far, none of the other three have admitted it was them."

"Could there be a fifth man?"

Cousin Cordelia inhaled sharply with umbrage. "*Five* men?"

"A fifth man for Fridays?" Benny posed with an amused look. "Perhaps that's where she was off to last week?"

"So why is there no evidence of him? At least beyond that card we found in her apartment."

"Perhaps she wasn't paying him?" Jane asked innocently enough. Benny coughed out a laugh, which made her realize how that sounded.

"Well, he obviously doesn't care about her, does he? At least with the others, she had something to show for it, beautiful paintings, delightful figurines, books, and music."

"The flowers," Pen said, she shot up from her seat without another word and rushed out of the apartment. She was smart enough to take the service elevator down to the first floor. Unfortunately, that meant a winding way to get to the lobby, so she took the exit and skittered down the sidewalk and around to go through the front doors.

She was just in time.

"Rodney, I'm glad I caught you," she said, slightly breathless as she addressed the doorman who was just about to end his morning shift and allow Eugene to take over for the afternoon. "Friday morning, did Mrs. Abernathy receive flowers?"

His expression became somber at the name, as he'd apparently been appraised of her murder. "Yes, she did.

Quite a few bouquets of roses. I suppose it was nice she had some bit of joy before the worst happened."

"Was it only roses? No other flowers were delivered that day?"

"Only roses."

"No deliveries? No lavender? No hydrangeas?"

"Not on my watch at any rate."

"Mine either," Eugene said.

"Perhaps on Thursday or another day?"

Both of them shook their heads no. Stephen worked overnight when no deliveries were likely to have been made.

"And you didn't see her bring them in herself?"

Again they both shook their heads no.

"So whoever brought them, would have had to come in through the service entrance."

"Well, they'd need a key, then, wouldn't they?"

"Or followed someone in? They could have possibly picked the lock as well." Pen thought it over. She was almost certain this fifth mysterious beau was the one who'd sent roses. That many would have been expensive, especially that time of year. He was also the one Mrs. Abernathy was most likely traveling with. But had he been the one to murder her?

More importantly, who was he?

She knew one place to look. "Thank you both."

Pen sighed, realizing she'd have to take the main elevator up. She used the time inside to consider that new development. The roses had looked rather fresh, perhaps only a few days old. Had this fifth man used them as bait to beguile poor Mrs. Abernathy and lure her out of the apartment to visit him? Or was it whoever had brought her the lavender and hydrangeas?

Back in the apartment, she ignored the questions from everyone else and instead rushed to the phone. Richard would be at the station, so she called his number there.

"Richard," she blurted before he could even get a word in. "I think there's a fifth man. The one she was going to Europe with. Has anyone reported her missing or called to inquire about her?"

There was silence on the other end before she heard him breathe out a long slow breath. "That mind of yours, sometimes I wonder if it's omniscient as well."

"What do you mean?"

"A Jacob Millington came by about an hour ago. He'd read about her in the evening paper last night. Apparently, they were childhood friends who had only recently begun a more personal relationship, both of them having been widowed."

"And he came by only today?" If Mrs. Abernathy had been on her way to see him Friday why had he only come to the police that day?

"To answer the question I know you're going to ask— the same one I had—he hadn't reported her missing sooner because he assumed she had changed her mind about being with him. He claims he sent the roses that Friday morning to reassure her where his heart lay. He said she was going to move in with him before their grand adventure overseas."

"And he didn't bother checking to see if perhaps something had happened to her before now?"

"I think you need to factor in a man's pride, Penelope. You saw how many roses there were in the apartment. To make such a grand gesture only to be met with silence?"

"Well, I certainly hope if you ever make any grand gestures and I don't respond you won't assume I'm being a stubborn prima donna in an attempt to make you beg even more. Rest assured I'd be lying dead in Central Park."

"That thought is quite reassuring, Penelope," he said in a cynical tone.

She smiled to herself. "You know what I mean. Still, do you think I could have his information so—"

"No. I'm not in the business of handing out personal information about New York's residents. Besides, he does have an alibi. He'd been waiting patiently in the Oak Room at the Plaza Hotel all afternoon. I checked and confirmed with the staff myself."

"All afternoon?"

"He's a romantic, I suppose."

"Well, I suppose *I'll* just have to use my investigative abilities to get his information. Just to be sure, of course."

"Your confidence in my occupational abilities is always so reassuring, my dear."

"It's not you that I don't trust, it's the constraints of your profession."

"You mean ethics, morals, rules, regulations? Things like that?"

"Yes," she said briskly.

"And did you find anything useful during your unburdened investigation?"

Pen told him everything that had happened that morning, including the dog's reaction to each man, at least those she could get them close enough to.

"So it may have been this Mr. Comeau who attacked you?" She could hear the angry edge in his voice. No, Detective Prescott would never simply accept her silence. He'd come looking for her.

"Or perhaps he really did trip and hurt himself. I still need to get them close to Beau. He was a little too smug this morning. Alan as well. As for Percy, I'm still uncertain about him. Despite his rather effeminate affect, Benny swears he isn't that way. I think the money would have been the lure for him. Which doesn't take him out of the running for her murder."

"Right," he said thoughtfully.

"At any rate, tonight Benny's taking me somewhere that may eliminate at least one suspect. My ethics, morals, rules, and regulations prohibit me from saying where."

"That fills me with concern. And I don't trust Benny to throw a punch for you if need be."

Pen laughed. "Why detective, I'm perfectly able to throw my own punches. Besides, I doubt I'll run into trouble at that sort of place."

"Should I ask what you'll be up to in the meantime?"

"I could tell you, but then you'd have to arrest me."

"Something tells me I should do that anyway for your own good."

"Detective," Pen said in faux outrage. "The dogs are right here. By now, I'm sure they're quite scandalized."

He laughed. "Just be careful, my dear."

"I will, darling," Pen said, still feeling that flutter in her stomach every time he called her "my dear."

They said their goodbyes.

"So, what did he say?"

"Why did you leave so suddenly?"

"What is going on?"

Pen turned to Cousin Cordelia, Jane, and Benny with a grin. "I just discovered our fifth mystery man. And I know exactly how to find him."

CHAPTER TWENTY-ONE

Despite the protests of her partners in private investigating—or perhaps partners in crime, considering the slightly unethical thing she was about to do—Penelope insisted she had to work alone in her plan to get Jacob Millington's information.

She pleasantly trotted along 5th Avenue until she reached the Plaza Hotel, which was only a few blocks south of the Alstonian. Once in the lobby, she erased the smile and planted a determined expression on her face as she strutted purposefully to the front desk.

"Hello, welcome to The Plaza Hotel."

"I'm desperately hoping you can help me. I have a letter for one of your guests. A Mr. Jacob Millington?"

"Of course. Let me just check to see if he is staying with us." The young man who greeted her kept a professional smile on his face as he searched their guest book. She wasn't surprised when it faded, telling her what she already knew. Pen certainly hadn't expected that Mr. Millington would still have a room there. But she suspected he had on Friday. At least he had if Mrs. Abernathy was going out the past few Fridays, and not returning until the next morning as Eugene had hinted. "Oh, I'm afraid we don't have a Mr. Millington currently staying with us."

"You don't?" Pen asked, a disheartened expression coming to her face. "But I was assured he was staying here. It's very important that he gets this letter and the only information I have is that he's a guest here at The Plaza. He *has* to be here. Can you check your book again and make sure? Perhaps he was staying here earlier and someone made a mistake?"

He made a show of flipping the pages and studying each one, most likely to appease her. Penelope surreptitiously committed each page to memory as he did.

As tactful as ever, the young man forced a smile to his face as he responded. "I'm very sorry, but if he was a guest, I can assure you that he no longer is."

"Of course you can't say so," she conceded, giving him a reassuring smile. "I suppose I'll have to simply tell my boss that the information we received about him was wrong. Thank you so much for your help."

Penelope left quickly before he could offer something problematic like mailing the letter for her. Still, she was pleased that she had in fact nabbed Mr. Millington's address from the second page to which the unsuspecting young man at the front desk had flipped. Yes, it was upside down in her head, but at least it was there.

She was beaming when she returned to her apartment. "It seems we have another little trip to make, this time across town. Our fifth man lives on the West Side, a very chic address I might add. This should be interesting."

"Oh?" Cousin Cordelia said, looking highly interested.

"This is for work, Cousin."

"I don't see why I can't simply go and wait in the car, perhaps? After all, Benny doesn't work for you either."

"No, I'm going purely out of nosiness."

Pen gave him an exasperated look. "Thank you for that."

He shrugged.

"Then I most certainly get to go as well," Cousin Cordelia said with a firm set to her mouth.

"Fine, you can be in charge of Dot and Dash."

"You're taking them?"

"They, unlike certain people—" She gave Benny a hard look. "—will actually serve some purpose in all of this."

"I'll be in charge of Dot and Dash," Jane offered, ever the voice of peace. "It's a big car, enough to carry us all."

"There then, it's settled," Cousin Cordelia said, as though it were.

"Fine, fine!" Pen said, throwing up her hands. It wasn't worth the fight. Perhaps this Mr. Millington would say something so unsavory that her cousin would forever be dissuaded from wanting to join in on an investigation.

It was a crowded ride across town. They did seem rather like an act in a circus with three women in heavy coats, two dogs, and two men. Dot and Dash, who had taken a nice nap over lunch—Little Monster had learned to flee when they wanted their beds—were full of energy once again, tails eagerly wagging, unconcerned as to whom they hit in the face. It was the very reason Pen had chosen the side window view.

Leonard came to a stop in front of an elegant townhouse that suggested money.

"It would seem it wasn't only, *ahem*, working men that the dearly departed Mrs. Abernathy was involved with."

"Stop Benny. We have to assume he's in mourning," Pen

said, opening her car door before Leonard could. She was eager to meet this Mr. Millington.

The others piled out, presenting a perfect spectacle for anyone watching through their windows on the quiet street. Thank goodness the car was tony and they were well dressed enough not to raise too much suspicion. Penelope led the charge up the steps to the front door. Benny was close behind. Jane was practically dragged along by the dogs. Cousin Cordelia brought up the rear, not wanting to seem too intrusive—or perhaps keeping a wide berth of the dogs who had already assaulted her with their tails in the car.

Once Dot and Dash were standing right on the top step next to her, poised to give their reaction once the door was answered, Penelope rang the doorbell.

CHAPTER TWENTY-TWO

The door to Mr. Jacob Millington's home was answered by a butler, which Penelope fully expected. She could only imagine what a sight her cadre made—two dogs, Jane, Benny, Cousin Cordelia, and Pen, all crowded on the steps.

"Hello, my name is Miss Penelope Banks. I have an urgent matter to discuss with Mr. Millington regarding Dorothy Abernathy?"

She hoped that would at least spur an invitation inside once the butler relayed the news to his employer.

"Did you say you were Miss Penelope Banks?"

"Yes?"

"Ah, Mr. Millington has been expecting you."

All the occupants on the front steps stared back perfectly dumbfounded. Everyone except for Dot and Dash. They began barking, tugging at the leash that Jane desperately tried to hold onto. That was enough to snap Penelope out of her surprise and narrow her eyes with suspicion. At least until she heard a bark from somewhere inside the home. One moment later, a Dalmatian came bounding out to the steps, nearly crashing into Dot and Dash. The three dogs greeted each other like old friends.

"A third Dalmatian?" Jane exclaimed.

"Please do come in," the butler said, though he cast an uncertain look past her at everyone else.

They crowded into the foyer to wait while the butler informed Mr. Millington that Penelope had arrived with guests. But how did he know she would be coming at all?

The butler returned. "If you would all please follow me."

They followed him into a parlor, very nicely done. The man seated in an armchair stood to greet them with a wan smile. Jacob Millington looked to be the same age as the late Mrs. Abernathy. He had regular features that didn't necessarily make him handsome, particularly in comparison to her other "acquaintances." In fact, everything about him was perfectly average, average height, medium build; even his hair was a salt and pepper that hadn't gone fully gray. Still, he had a warm and welcoming presence.

His eyes flicked past Penelope, who had entered first, to the others with her, then down to the dogs. "I see Roger has wasted no time greeting his sisters."

"Sisters?" Jane practically squealed.

"Yes, they all came from the same litter."

"So it seems you've known Mrs. Abernathy for some time then," Pen said. "But how exactly did you know I was coming?"

"Detective Prescott mentioned that I might be visited by a Miss Penelope Banks. He stated you were a private investigator. That I should work with you if I wanted to help find out what had happened to Dorothy."

"Did he?" Penelope was surprised. Their conversation had led her to believe he wanted her to have nothing to do with this case. She would have to thank him properly when this was all over. Or perhaps give him a good what's for, making her work so hard to get Mr. Millington's information when he could have just told her.

"I apologize, I'm being quite rude. Do please sit down." He gestured to the seating in the parlor. "I hadn't expected quite so many people to join you."

"These are my associates. And Dot and Dash, we brought along for different reasons."

"I'm glad you did," he said, looking over at all three dogs fondly. A sad expression befell him. "I had hoped they'd be reunited under happier circumstances."

He looked genuinely grief-stricken. Still, Pen couldn't get past how long he'd waited to inquire about Mrs. Abernathy.

"How did you know Mrs. Abernathy?"

He brought his attention back to her. "We were child-hood friends—perhaps more than friends at one point. Everyone assumed we would get married. *I* had certainly assumed so. Then...Spencer blew in." He looked thought-fully off to the side. "I don't fault Dorothy for being overly impressed by him. She was always far more adventurous, vivacious, and even a bit rebellious than I'd ever been. And Spencer had a reckless spirit about him that she fell in love with. He had money, certainly, and he was handsome, but also...he had a presence. It impressed everyone, even me in a way. But he wanted Dorothy, and so she was his."

He sighed, before continuing. "I could see right away what life with him would be like for her. That everything she was attracted to would eventually tarnish and the marriage would be nothing short of a prison. They had nothing in common, he was a braggart and a bore. He had no interest in things like art and dancing, both of which she loved. She told me their wedding was the last time she had ever danced with him."

Pen thought back to the half-empty bookshelf. Jacob's description of Spencer fit with the titles that remained, all plots dedicated to men's fantasies of adventure and danger.

"Still, once her vows were exchanged, I knew I had to move on. Don't get me wrong, Albertha was the most wonderful wife any man could have asked for, and I loved her dearly. I don't regret marrying her at all. When she died in January last year, I mourned her loss quite heavily."

"How did you and Mrs. Abernathy reconnect?"

He smiled. "We had run into each other over the years. Coming from the same background and socializing in the same circles here in New York, that was inevitable. I, of course, reached out directly when Spencer died. I was the one to suggest she adopt Dot and Dash. She'd had a Dalmatian growing up. Roger's mother had just produced a fine litter and she opted for two of his sisters. I took Roger, as the dog my wife and I owned had recently passed.

"One could say it might have been fate. When Albertha died, it was Dorothy's turn to reach out to me. It started as a friendship, quite innocent. We'd meet for tea, or go to museums, and reminisce about our youth. She never broached the idea of picking up where we had once left off. To be fair, I wasn't ready for anything more, as I was still mourning, and told her as much. I knew she was romantically involved with other men and I certainly didn't fault her. It was a terrible marriage she'd had, and she had every right to make up for lost time when it came to romance.

"Then, only recently, it changed. For both of us. She claimed she was done with frivolous men and meaningless relationships that would never amount to anything serious. I had finally decided to move on, as Albertha would have wanted me to do."

"She invited you to join her in Europe?" Pen asked.

"Yes," he said thoughtfully. "But I didn't say yes right away. I didn't want us trotting off to Europe only for her to become bored of me and move on. I told her if we were going to do this, we couldn't do it on a whim, that I'd want her to move in with me first to make sure we were compatible. I realize it's a modern age, where that kind of thing isn't so scandalous. Still, I think she was rather hesitant to tell anyone about it. I still deemed it a necessary first step, and she had agreed."

That explained the packed trunks, and the fact that not even her staff seemed to know the details.

"This is going to sound a bit insensitive but did she consider taking someone other than you beforehand?"

"Not that I know of. She had made it quite clear that she planned on ending any further social involvement with those other men. In fact, she seemed particularly upset about one of them. She told me she had been betrayed by him, that he hadn't been honest with her, and she had proof. She planned to do something about it before we left."

Penelope perked up. "But she didn't say who it was?"

He shook his head. "I'm afraid not. I think she was embarrassed over the whole ordeal. I didn't push, not wanting to cause her further embarrassment. Now, I wonder if..."

He obviously had the same thought Pen did, that whoever this man was, he'd been the one to lure her into the park and kill her, perhaps to keep her quiet.

Or perhaps he was lying?

"Again, I hate to ask, but Mrs. Abernathy was apparently killed on Friday. I'm just wondering why—"

"Why I waited so long to inquire with the police?"

"Yes."

He nodded as though he fully understood why she had asked. There was a long pause before he answered. "We had gotten into a fight that week. Dorothy was so upset about this man, how she hadn't been the only woman who had been lured in by his charms and bona fides, only to have been taken. I told her she should let it go, move on with her life—with *our* life. That she should simply go to the police and allow them to handle it. But she didn't want to involve them, said it would only humiliate those other women. It was getting to the point where it was all she could talk about. I told her to deal with it how she saw fit, and do what she needed to do to move on. That I was tired of seeing her obsess over it. That when she was done, she could come back to me, and we could finally move on, begin our life together." He paused, swallowing hard. "That was Thursday."

"So you didn't communicate with her in any way after that?"

He gave Pen a sheepish look, which was rather endearing for a man his age. "I sent roses, a lot of them—perhaps too many. I knew how much flowers meant to Dorothy. Spencer never sent her flowers, thought it was a foolish expenditure. He lavished her with jewels—" He laughed softly, sadly. "—which she also loved, of course. Wearing them made her happy, which in turn made me happy. However, to show her commitment, she claimed she would be selling them off, every piece he'd ever given her. She didn't want any reminders of him ruining things between us."

Pen heard Jane and Cousin Cordelia next to her both sigh at that.

"Dorothy was a romantic at heart. Flowers were what she valued most, even more than jewelry. She loved the subtle ways they sent messages. So I sent red roses, to represent love, of course; baby's breath was for everlasting love. I also sent a note with them, apologizing and letting her know that I would be at The Plaza that afternoon. That I'd be waiting there for her. We had been meeting there on Fridays you see, spending the night."

He showed no shame about that. Those were modern times after all.

"Thus, when she didn't respond or show up, I thought perhaps she was..."

"I see," Pen said, saving him from having to say that he thought Mrs. Abernathy was simply playing hard to get.

"I must admit, a part of me was irritated. I had thought those games of ours were over and done with. I figured being stubborn myself might make her realize what a wound it causes to the one you supposedly care for." His face crumpled. "Then I saw the paper this morning."

There was a moment of awkwardness when he succumbed to tears. It was brief, and a crooked smile of embarrassment came to his face, all the more so because of the audience in front of him. "I apologize for that. I suppose I'm an emotional sort of man. It's just, thinking of her lying dead in the park, while I was being a stubborn fool."

"If it helps, I don't think you trying to reach out sooner would have helped. I suspect she was lured into the park by one of these other men."

He nodded.

"So you only sent roses? No lavender or hydrangeas?"

"Goodness no," he said, looking slightly alarmed. "Apart from the meaning they would impart—"

At Pen's questioning look, he explained.

"Dorothy was faithful to the Victorian interpretation of flowers. We are products of that time period, after all. Hydrangeas represent boastfulness, bragging, or vanity. When we were younger, the girls would carry small nosegays with them if they wanted to taunt another girl with some bit of triumph. Certainly not something I would send to her.

"As for lavender, well that's so much more sinister. In our day, the legend was that the asp that killed Cleopatra hid under a lavender bush. If your intent is to scare someone off, or suggest a threat, it was the perfect flower. Furthermore, both flowers are highly toxic to dogs. Don't tell me she had lavender and hydrangeas in her apartment?"

"There was a vase full of them right on display in the living room."

His gaze darted to the three dogs who had settled into a corner with one another. "Thank goodness nothing happened to either of them. I can't imagine Dorothy keeping such flowers in the apartment. And anyone sending them to her should have known better."

"Unless their intent was to send a sinister message."

Everyone in the room was silent, absorbing that somber thought.

"Did Mrs. Abernathy tell you what she planned to do about this man she thought had betrayed her?"

"No, she knew I had no interest in hearing about it." He sighed and looked morose. He didn't need to express yet again his regrets at things he could have possibly done to change the outcome. Pen didn't think it would have mattered either way.

It was beginning to look more and more like Mrs. Abernathy's death was premeditated.

"Thank you for your time, Mr. Millington," Penelope

said, rising from the couch. She reached into her purse to pull out a business card to hand to him. "If you think of anything that might help identify who it was Mrs. Abernathy was targeting, please call me."

"Of course," he said, rising to take hold of it.

"One more thing, had Mrs. Abernathy planned to take Dot and Dash with you to Europe?"

"Yes, and Roger of course." He laughed. "It was mad, but we wouldn't have dreamt of leaving them behind. When you have money, people tend to accommodate you *and* your dogs. In fact, I had already bought far too much dog food in preparation for her staying with me. All she had to do was move in. That was before our little spat, of course."

"Of course. Thank you for your time. You have my condolences, Mr. Millington," Pen said before they all left.

"So do we believe him?" Benny asked once they were crowded back in the car.

"He was awfully convincing," Pen said. Her years playing poker and other card games to make extra money had taught her how to read a poker face. "Also, I don't really see a motive. He knew about the other men, and everything fits with her ending things with them."

"Unless there's a sixth man," Cousin Cordelia scoffed, the sides of her mouth turned down with disapproval.

"That sounds like a lot to juggle," Jane said.

Benny laughed. "Yes, it does."

"Let's go back to the apartment. I need to make a phone call to Detective Prescott." For a number of reasons, Pen thought to herself.

CHAPTER TWENTY-THREE

I n the car on the way back from Jacob Millington's home, everyone was still abuzz with the question: which of Mrs. Abernathy's other suitors she had planned on exposing?

"Frankly, they all seem suspicious to me," Benny said.

"Yes, I think they all might have something to hide," Pen agreed. "Beau seems to have a penchant for targeting wealthy, enamored women. He also claimed she had initially invited him to go with her to Europe and he passed. Why would he lie about that? Maybe he was upset she hadn't asked him? After all, the patronage of a woman like her would have been far more valuable to his career than teaching a class, never mind the sort of people she could've introduced him to."

"Then there's Alan Lashbrook." She darted her eyes over Dash's head toward Cousin Cordelia. "I suspect the same was true of him. It must be tiring charming his way through multiple women every day. I know I'd rather be in a first-class cabin on the Atlantic."

Penelope quickly moved on. "As for Taylor Comeau,

well, he was most definitely undervaluing all of her late husband's books, I'm sure of it. He was probably doing the same to many other widows. Then there's Percy Dawson. I'm certain he was involved in that business you were talking about, Leonard, with the fake Lachapelles?"

"There were fakes?" Cousin Cordelia said, a look of astonishment on her face.

The fact that she hadn't heard about it circulating among her friends told Pen that it had indeed been kept secret. No one wanted to admit they had been taken. One of Cousin Cordelia's most highly honed assets was a nose for gossip. She would have reveled in the idea that a wealthy member of New York's elite had been fooled by a fake Lachapelle.

"His business already seems to have suffered from the fallout. If he'd been outed as the maestro who had coordinated those fakes in the first place, he'd be facing prison. At the very least, his exclusive contract to sell along the East Coast would have been ripped from him."

"The dirty rat!" Cousin Cordelia said.

"We don't know for sure he was involved," Jane cautioned.

"And he certainly isn't going to admit it if we question him."

"That's why I want to talk to Mrs. Abernathy's former maid and cook. Someone had to have let in whoever delivered that bouquet of lavender and hydrangeas."

The car was silent for a moment to register that.

"Do you think it was an inside job?" Cousin Cordelia was the one to finally ask.

"That's what I intend to find out."

When they got back to the apartment, it was well after five, thanks to New York traffic. Their arrival coincided with Alice and Walter stepping out of a taxi together. They both looked startled to have been discovered, all the more so at Pen's knowing grin.

"I offered to pick Alice up from work and escort her here, for her own safety," Walter said, the usual tinge of red coming to his face.

"I thought it was a very kind gesture," Alice said, flashing a quick look of ardor his way.

"I heartily agree," Pen said. She looked down at Dot and Dash, who were eagerly pulling at their leashes to greet their favorite person. "These two have had quite the day, though it seems we haven't completely worn them out."

"Well, I think we can manage that, can't we girls?" Alice said, her self-consciousness disappearing as she leaned over to scratch behind their ears. Even Walter seemed to have warmed to them.

After the rather suffocating and chaotic car ride back to the apartment from the West Side—it sometimes boggled her mind how long it took to travel from one side of New York to the other—Pen wasn't ashamed to breathe a sigh of temporary relief as the two dogs led Alice and Walter away. She was certain Leonard would quit on the spot if that became a habit.

Pen didn't even mind the slow elevator ride up to the eleventh floor, as weary as she was from the busy day. A bit of vim returned once she was in the apartment. After depositing her coat and hat with Chives, she stalked right over to the phone to call Richard. Fortunately, he was still at his desk, which only made sense, since he was working on an active murder investigation.

"If you were going to tell Jacob Millington that I was coming, the least you could have done was give me the address," Penelope scolded as soon as he answered.

"I told you why I couldn't. Besides, I had every faith in your ability to discover it on your own, and it seems I was right. Dare I ask how you accomplished that small feat?"

"Do you really want to know?"

"I suppose not. So, did you learn anything useful?"

"Nothing you didn't already know, apparently, which you also didn't tell me about."

"I didn't?"

"No, and don't play the forgetful dunce with me. It was important information."

"Which is exactly why I thought you should hear it from him in person. There are certain things one can only pick up by talking to someone face to face, which I'm sure you discovered."

"Well, yes, I suppose." He did have a point. "So you don't think he's guilty of anything?"

"I'm guessing you don't either, considering the way the question was posed."

"No, but I've been fooled at least once before. It's a compelling story," she conceded, then quickly moved on to why she had called. "But I did learn something that I'd like to check on."

She told him about what Jacob had said about the lavender and hydrangeas.

"Someone had to have either accepted delivery of them or brought them in directly after she was murdered. According to him, she wouldn't have allowed such flowers in the house. I'd like to speak to her maid or cook to find out if they were there that afternoon, or sometime this past weekend."

"Perhaps that explains why the dogs were sick. Still, they were in a vase on a table. Maybe they jumped up on the table in the library and ate some?" Richard sounded doubtful.

"Not very smart of them," Pen said skeptically. "All the more reason to talk to either Sally or Martha. As you stated, face-to-face is better than hearing things secondhand. And please don't make me go through another case of legally questionable means to obtain the information, which you know I'll get either way."

He sighed. "It's easily available from the agency they went through so I suppose I'll save you the trouble." He gave her the information, which she wrote down, in order to commit to memory in her head.

"Walter, her nephew, said you wanted him to go through the apartment to see if anything was missing?"

"He told you that?"

"Yes, I saw him this morning when he came by to do it."

"Well, he hasn't called to report back yet."

"He may have been a bit preoccupied with more impor-tant endeavors," Pen said, a smile coming to her face. "He offered to go with Alice as she took Dot and Dash on their walks."

"I see," he said in a knowing tone. "It seems someone has been playing Cupid."

"I can't help it if two people are obviously meant for one another. I do so love conflicting personalities coming together that way."

He laughed. "Of course you do."

"Not to worry, he promised to do it as soon as they get back." She heard the door opening as they returned. "And here they are. You should be getting that phone call soon enough."

"I'll be here for a while longer anyway. Just have him call me at the station."

"Aye, aye, detective."

They both laughed and hung up.

Penelope followed Alice and the dogs into the living room, where everyone else had settled. Benny had already helped himself to a cocktail from her bar. Cousin Cordelia frowned at the overly active dogs while petting the equally unamused Lady Dinah on her lap. Little Monster fought a losing battle with the dogs for the beds, settling on forcing his way into a warm little crook between Dot's legs as she lay down.

"Walter is in Mrs. Abernathy's apartment, checking for anything missing," Alice said with cheeks that were still rosy.

"Did Detective Prescott tell you anything?" Jane asked.

Pen decided to first tell Alice about everything they'd learned that day. She was particularly affected by the news regarding Mr. Millington.

"So after all this time, they're finally reunited only for her to be killed just before they run off together?" Pen thought she would cry, she was such an emotional young thing. "And Dot and Dash eating those flowers? Yes, that would have certainly made them sick, possibly even killed them!"

"I really would like to talk to her former maid. She would have been the one most likely to open the door to someone."

"Don't forget our little adventure this evening," Benny reminded her. "The, ahem, club should start populating about now."

"Yes, but it's better to have a timeline of events from Friday. Sally may even know the identity of the man who brought the toxic flowers."

"She really should have known better. Mrs. Abernathy was quite strict about that. She knew all about flowers."

"Let's just hope it was an oversight on her part and not intentional, if indeed she was the one to do it."

There was a knock on the front door and Chives opened it. Walter rushed in with an anxious look on his face. "I did a thorough check. I'm not that familiar with Aunt Dorothy's apartment, but I did specifically search for valuables I know she owns. The thing is, I can't seem to find any of the jewelry Uncle Spencer gave her."

CHAPTER TWENTY-FOUR

Penelope told Jane to go home lest Alfie give her an earful for being a tyrant of a boss. After being in charge of the dogs all day, she looked exhausted. Richard had come as quickly as possible after Walter had called to tell him that he couldn't find any of his aunt's jewelry.

Walter led Detective Prescott through the apartment to do a more thorough inspection and they both came back to Pen's place with the same conclusion: the jewelry was gone.

Alice had never seen the apartment beyond the common rooms, so she wouldn't have known where the valuables were usually stored.

"All the more reason to talk to Sally, the maid. She'd certainly know where they would be." Pen said.

"Or she took the jewels herself," Benny offered as though that was obvious.

"At this point, I agree with you, Penelope," Richard said. "In the meantime, Mr. Abernathy, if you could write down a description of every piece you remember? Miss

Winterfort, since you may have seen her wearing some of it, could you work with him?"

Alice and Walter both stared wide-eyed for a moment before nodding and inadvertently stepping closer to one another.

"Very subtle," Penelope murmured as Richard and she went to the foyer to retrieve their coats and hats before leaving.

"What?" Richard responded, shooting her an innocent look. "You aren't the only one who can play Cupid. Besides, she probably *could* offer assistance, seeing as she was at the apartment twice a day. She must have seen something."

"Mmm-hmm, Mr. Matchmaker," Pen teased with a laugh as they left.

Sally's new home of employment was a townhouse further north, blessedly on the East Side of Manhattan. Like many such buildings, there was a separate entrance for staff below the front stairs. Richard and Penelope knocked on that door, rather than alert the occupants of the main house to their visit. No need to raise questions or eyebrows just when she had started employment.

The cook was the one to answer, giving Penelope in particular a wary look as she eyed her fine coat and hat. "Can I help you?"

"I'm Detective Prescott, here to speak with Sally Mayfair. I need to ask her about something she may have accidentally witnessed," he added.

The qualifier did nothing to alleviate the look of suspicion on her face. "Sally's attending to her duties right now. I'll fetch Henson, he'll know what to do about this." She paused before opening the door wider for them to step in so they wouldn't have to wait in the cold.

They respectfully waited in the tiny entry rather than fully invade the staff area. A moment later a dignified butler approached them with a pleasant but inquiring expression. "I understand you're looking for Sally?"

Richard showed his badge, which Henson dutifully inspected. "It shouldn't take more than about five minutes. She may have witnessed something that will assist in a case of mine."

Henson deliberately set his eyes on Penelope with an inquiring look.

"I'm Miss Banks. Also a witness," she fibbed. It wouldn't have done Sally any favors to have both a detective and a private investigator land on her doorstep asking questions.

"Very good," Henson said. "She's finishing up in the bedroom upstairs, but I instructed her to come down once she's finished. Perhaps you'd like to use my room for a bit of privacy?"

It was a request more than an offer, but they agreed in an appreciative manner. Henson probably didn't want to get the gossip mill going by having his staff overhear the details of whatever crime they were investigating. Or perhaps he suspected there may have been more to Sally's involvement than that of a mere witness.

They went into the room. A few minutes later there was a brief knock on the door before Sally appeared, looking perfectly put out. She had dark hair cut into a bob, much like Penelope's, and dark eyes that stared at them with irritation.

"I already told you everything I know," she said with a

stubborn set to her mouth. "I'm on probation still. This doesn't look good for me."

"I apologize for that Miss Mayfair. We had one more important inquiry to make," Richard said before turning to allow Penelope to speak.

"Your last day was this past Friday, correct?"

Sally hesitated, her eyes narrowing before she answered. "Yes."

"Did someone come by to deliver a vase of lavender and hydrangeas in the library before you left for good?"

She didn't answer right away, and Penelope could see in her eyes that she was working out what to say.

"You're not in any trouble," Pen said, if only to reassure her.

It was the wrong thing to say. Sally stood up straighter with indignation. "Why would I be in any trouble?"

"You wouldn't?" Pen said uncertainly.

"Did Martha say something? She's got a lot of nerve, that one."

"She may have mentioned something, but we just want to make certain it wasn't idle gossip, or the chatter of someone who might want to cause trouble." Again, it was a fib, but if it got her talking, Pen was willing to commit the sin.

"I knew it!" Sally hissed. "I figured she would come back for them, and sure enough... You listen to me, I only took them because they were still there. It wasn't as though Mrs. Abernathy was even using them. It's not theft or robbery, is it? I tell you, rich people don't even know the value of things. God rest her soul, of course."

Pen and Richard looked at one another in surprise then turned back to Sally.

"What is it you took?" Richard asked.

Sally's eyes squinted with suspicion. "What is it you think I took?"

"Please answer the question."

"You can't arrest me for it. They would have only gone to waste if not for me."

"What would have gone to waste?" Pen asked in exasperation.

Sally stuck her lower lip out further. "The cans of dog food, of course. I saw Martha had left them. Is she saying I took something else? Why, that conniving—"

"We aren't concerned about the dog food, Miss Mayfair," Richard said. "What time did you return to get it?"

"Around five o'clock that evening."

"Did you at least give Dot and Dash some food before you took it all?" Pen couldn't help but ask.

Sally gave her an impatient look. "They already had food. But it's a good thing I did go back that night, or those fool dogs would have killed themselves, what with—" She stopped, realizing she may have said too much.

Richard held his hands up in reassurance. "Miss Mayfair, I'm not going to arrest you for taking the dog food. Just please walk me through what happened that afternoon and evening."

"I don't know. Maybe I should talk to a lawyer?"

"Which is your right, if you'd like to call him or her?" Richard offered in a congenial tone.

Sally worked her jaw and glared at him. They all knew full well she didn't have an attorney.

"We're looking at someone else for the crime. One of the men Mrs. Abernathy may have been associating with. We think he was the one to kill her, but we need your help."

There was an amused gleam in Sally's eye at the

mention of the men in Mrs. Abernathy's life. She sniffed and lifted her chin loftily. "I suppose, so long as I'm not in any trouble, mind you."

"If your only crime is taking the dog food, then no, you aren't in any trouble as far as I'm concerned," Richard said.

"Right, well, I went back that night, going through the service entrance as usual. Martha had packed up and left before me, leaving the dog food. That was after she'd taken practically everything else in the kitchen. It's no wonder she's a porky one." Sally smoothed a hand over her slim figure. "She *said* she was taking it all to her sister, but I know better. Anyway, I guess her *sister* didn't have any use for those cans of dog food. Neither did I, until I came here and realized they have two dogs. I thought it would do me a bit of goodwill to bring them, as a kind of present or something. After all, Mrs. Abernathy did say to take everything in the kitchen, and those cans were in the kitchen."

She looked to them for confirmation.

"Go on," Richard said.

"Well, I went back later that night around five, as I said. I didn't tell you because you had only asked about the afternoon," she said, giving Richard a squinty-eyed look. "Mrs. Abernathy had been spending her nights elsewhere the past few Fridays, and I figured that night would be no different. I was right." She said with a wicked smirk.

"Go on," Penelope said. "What did you find when you got there?"

"Those two dogs were moaning and whining. I figured they wanted to go out for their walk, which I wasn't about to do, seeing as how I wasn't employed there anymore. Still, I figured I could at least put more water in their bowls. Well, I got to that part of the kitchen and I see the disgusting mess they had made in the corner. Again, no longer my job to clean that up, thank you very much, even if it did stink to high heaven. I was all set to leave when I saw what was in their bowls. Some idiot had put flower petals in with their food."

"Lavender or hydrangea?" Pen asked.

"Both, it looked like it. It was no wonder they had been sick, the silly dogs had gone and eaten it. I figured the least I should do was empty it out before they ate any more and killed themselves. Mrs. Abernathy, for all those flowers she had in the place all the time, was real strict about what we could and couldn't bring into the apartment and those were two of them."

"Did you put more food in for them after that?" Pen asked.

Sally gave her a cool look. "I thought they'd be too sick to eat that evening. No sense wasting food on them if all they were going to do was throw it back up. I figured one night without food couldn't hurt. Mrs. Abernathy always returned early enough in the morning. How was I to know she was already dead by then and wouldn't come back?"

Pen's mouth fell open. Before she could speak her mind, Richard placed a restraining hand on her arm.

"Of course you had no idea."

"Exactly," Sally said, giving Penelope a satisfied smile.

"So, it's safe to assume the bouquet of lavender and hydrangea was already in the apartment when you arrived?" Penelope asked in a dry tone.

"Yes, right there in the library. I figured they were safe enough high up on the table there. I assumed Mrs. Abernathy put them there. They were certainly pretty enough, and I knew she liked them. One of those paintings she had done included them."

So she hadn't been the one to let the flower deliverer in.

She'd also said Martha had packed up and left before her. That meant someone else had let themselves in—or broken in more likely—to do the dirty business of deliberately poisoning Mrs. Abernathy's dogs.

"Did anyone besides Martha, Alice, and you have a key to the apartment?"

"How would I know?"

"Do you know where Mrs. Abernathy kept her valuable jewelry?" Richard asked, moving on.

"I didn't take any jewelry!" Sally was understandably defensive. "How stupid do you think I am? I know the maid is the first person everyone suspects. What would I even do with all them jewels?"

"No one here is accusing you of stealing them, but it appears someone may have. Unless of course Mrs. Abernathy kept them someplace secret, somewhere anyone casually looking around wouldn't find them? Like a secret safe or hidden compartment?"

"No, she kept them right there in her closet. She had a large jewelry box, locked of course, a big shiny, wood thing."

They hadn't seen any wood box in the closet when they'd first looked.

"When you went back to get the dog food did you see if the box was still there?" Richard asked.

"I didn't go looking for it, so I wouldn't know," she said pointedly. "I was there for the dog food and that's it. Maybe you should be asking Martha where the jewels are. She was greedy enough to take all the food, maybe she got to thinking she'd take more than that?"

"Thank you for your time, Miss Mayfair."

Sally sniffed and glared at them, then left the butler's room without another word.

Richard and Penelope exited the building, returning to the cold evening air.

"I don't like her, but that hardly translates into her being a criminal," Pen confessed. "And I suppose if she hadn't gone back to take all the dog food, she might not have saved Dot and Dash from eating the rest of the poisoned food."

"The most likely candidate, who, at the very least, stole the jewelry is the person who brought the flowers. I'm thinking they entered your apartment building via the service entrance somehow, then made their way up to the eleventh floor. No one would look twice at a stranger delivering such a large bouquet, going up the service entrance, and down a hallway. Once there, he breaks in, puts the flowers in a vase, then steals the jewels...and decides to murder the dogs while he's at it? That means it's personal, somehow."

"Bastard," Penelope hissed, thinking of poor Dot and Dash. "But where was the jewelry box? We didn't find any when we looked around. I assume the police who did a more thorough search after her murder also didn't find it. Surely the thief didn't take it with him? That would have been both burdensome and conspicuous."

"The trash chute," Richard said, snapping his fingers as it hit him. "It's right there in the kitchen."

"Of course. Though, I imagine he wouldn't have been dumb enough to leave his prints on it before throwing it out. The good news is, the trash is collected on Thursdays, so it should still be there."

"I'll have the police go and search for it, just in case he *was* dumb enough to leave prints. You never know." Richard studied her. "I assume you'll be headed to your secret location with Benny?"

"Not to worry, my love," Pen said with a wink. "It's perfectly safe, I'm sure."

"I suppose I shouldn't ask too many questions, then," he said with a frown. "Just be careful."

"When am I not?"

"Should I answer that?"

She laughed and hooked her arm through his, headed back to his car. "It may eliminate a suspect in a case where there are far too many. Or, it may uncover our killer."

CHAPTER TWENTY-FIVE

Benny insisted that they take a taxi rather than have Leonard drive them to the private club where they would hopefully be learning more about Alan Lashbrook's whereabouts on Friday afternoon. He had the driver drop them off on a corner further down from the actual address. Benny waited until he had driven off before leading Penelope down the sidewalk. He stopped at a perfectly nondescript, three-story building that had only one black door.

Other than the number to the building and a side slot for mail, there was no indication as to what business took place inside. Though, as they got closer she could see that there was a small carved image to the right of the door. It was difficult to see with the street lighting being some distance from the front door—perhaps by design—but as she peered in, she could have sworn it looked like a small pansy.

"Fitting," she said with a grin.

"It's all the rage these days, don't you know," Benny said. He pulled a key out of his pocket. "At any rate, dove, this is where I bid you adieu. This is a gentlemen's club, after all."

"So much for modern times."

"I'll see what I can do to lure one of these fellows out to talk with you."

"Meanwhile, I'll try not to freeze to death," she groused, pulling her fur-lined coat more firmly around her.

He disappeared inside and she stood outside, feeling perfectly conspicuous. She laughed softly, the air turning to fog in front of her face, wondering if anyone passing might have thought she was a woman of the night. The idea tickled her until she saw a gentleman walking towards her from the corner. He was well-dressed, and as he passed, he gave her a deep frown of disapproval and continued on his way. It only occurred to her a moment later that perhaps he had wanted to go into the "pansy" club and she had been a risky witness.

Pen debated going to stand under the streetlight if only for her own safety, and the reassurance of any other patrons who would have liked to enter the club. That would have sent entirely the wrong message to the public. She laughed again at the idea of being arrested for solicitation. What would Richard have made of that?

The door opened and Pen was pleased to see Benny come out with another man, who himself didn't seem particularly pleased. He eyed Penelope up and down and gave her a look of utter disapproval.

"Can we please dispense with this quickly? It's cold as the devil out here," he said, even though he wore a fine sable coat, scarf, and a hat. Benny arched a brow and gave her an expectant look.

"Alan Lashbrook, was he here this past Friday?"

The man looked at Benny. "I have your assurance the police won't be involved?"

"Of course," Benny said with overt earnestness.

He pursed his lips and turned his attention back to Penelope. "He was, from noon until at least five."

"That long?"

He gave her a patronizing look. "It's a gentlemen's club. An escape from the world outside where one can converse and socialize with like-minded men. We offer all the same amenities, rooms for card games, a library, gymnasium, indoor pool, even a bar." He turned to give Benny a warning look, seeking reassurance that it was a strictly private conversation.

"Yes, but how do you know he was here that entire time?" Pen asked, drawing his attention back.

"I myself saw him come in and, later on, leave. At noon, we have a weekly meeting to discuss issues pertinent to us. Nothing political, mind you. We don't make those kinds of waves. I saw him there. That lasted until one. Then, I saw him in the study enjoying a cigar and...a drink." He cleared his throat at that, which told Pen it must have been alcohol. "That was until two or so. Then he went to the gym. I saw him come back later for another cigar and drink, then he left around five."

"So you didn't actually see him in the gym?"

"No, but one of our other members saw him in the locker room. Benjamin explained why it is you're asking these questions, Miss Banks. I find it highly unlikely that any *legitimate—*" He cast a harsh look Benjamin's way "—member of our club would have committed something as unsavory as murder. Further, as stated, I saw him after his return from the gym. That was about four-ish, and he certainly didn't have the look of someone who had just strangled a woman."

"But no one had eyes on him at all times."

"I'm sure if I ask around someone would have seen him at all times."

"Are there...private areas in the club, places where no one could see him?"

He glared at her. "This is *not* that sort of club, Miss Banks. Just because you young people have turned decent society into a debauched bacchanal doesn't mean the rest of us—yes, even those of us whom society frowns upon—have to do the same. There is something to be said for decorum, even simple gentility."

"I take it I won't be seeing you at the Hamilton Lodge for the Masquerade and Civic Ball this year, then?" Benny said in a droll voice.

Pen had no idea what that was, but from the perfect look of disdain on the man's face—it occurred to her he hadn't offered his name—it was probably a "debauched bacchanal."

She'd had her question answered and despite the man's beliefs, it was perfectly possible Alan had left and come back. There was a one-and-a-half to two-hour window where he could have slipped out and killed Mrs. Abernathy and returned. Still, Pen figured she should put the squeeze on while she had him.

"What *was* he like that afternoon? Did you talk to him at all?"

"Alan and I have little in common—besides the obvious. I have no interest whatsoever in the latest happenings among wealthy old women. Yes, there might have been the occasional interesting tidbit of gossip to be had. However, most of the time it wasn't worth filtering it through Alan grousing about the occupation that *he* had chosen, mind you. Quite the lucrative one if he has a key to get in here."

"Any interesting gossip of late?" Benny asked.

Pen gave him an impatient look and he shrugged, as though he couldn't help himself. Sometimes she thought he was worse than Cousin Cordelia.

"Nothing worth passing on."

"Had he been grousing about anything in particular lately?" Pen asked.

"The usual. How inept most of his students were at dancing. What a chore it was to maintain the charm through it all. How it was like pulling teeth to move them into more modern dances they had no interest in. I, for one, don't know why he doesn't stick to waltzes. Those lonely old women don't go to him to learn the Charleston. They want to feel like a princess."

"Don't we all?" Benny sang, much to the man's chagrin.

Penelope bit back a smile. "Thank you for your time."

Later that night, Pen was walking Dot and Dash with Richard. She clung to his side, mostly because of the sudden drop in temperature, but also the memories of what had happened the night before. She could see that he was more alert as well, his eyes darting back and forth into the darker areas of the park as they continued down the path.

At least Dot and Dash seemed at ease, which was reassuring. They served as wonderful warning bells, should someone try to attack again.

"Did you learn anything that you're able to tell me about Mr. Lashbrook?" Richard asked.

"Only that his alibi is flawed. There is a window where

he could have made it to the park near the Alstonian and killed Mrs. Abernathy. So, he's still on the list of suspects, though not at the top. That's reserved for Mr. Comeau. He has to be the one she was upset about. It's either him or Percy Dawson, who maintains the Lachapelle shop. I'm starting with them tomorrow."

"And I'm going with you. At this point, it makes sense to work together."

Pen was set to protest, but she couldn't find any reason for it. Perhaps it would be good to have a detective there, both of them using their respective advantages to flush out the culprit.

"Jane will like it at any rate. I assume you got your invitation to the wedding by now?"

He grinned. "Special delivery."

"I would have made you my plus one, but it seems I'm a maid of honor, which I think is wonderful. I've often been a bridesmaid, too often to count, but this is a rare treat. I'm glad she found Alfie."

"You should think about starting a side business in matchmaking. It seems you're rather good at it."

Pen laughed. "I'm even better at solving murders. I hope this one doesn't break my run of success in that area. I'm at that point in the case where I should feel as though something obvious is staring me in the face, and I just have to latch onto it. But I'm not there yet."

"It's only been two days since we learned it was murder, Penelope. Don't be so hard on yourself. I've had cases that took months to solve."

Pen frowned. She certainly didn't want it to take that long to find the killer. If only she could discover what made this case so different from her prior cases.

Perhaps the next day would shed some light on it.

CHAPTER TWENTY-SIX

The next day, Alice and Walter had taken Dot and Dash out together once again, then shared a taxi to their respective jobs.

Mrs. Abernathy's case had certainly created an air of suggestion. Pen could only hope she'd also leave such a legacy of scandal when she died.

When Richard came to her office, Benny was there again, much to Jane's delight. With his ribald tales, he was gradually replacing Detective Prescott as her favorite.

"Enough of that, you two. Today is the day we figure out what's going on with this case. There's something off about it, and I want to know why. Jane, I'd like you to stay here and make a few phone calls to make sure everyone was honest in what they told us. Start with Beau Blackman. Check the art school and make sure he really has a position as a teacher. If you can do it, subtly inquire as to any complaints students may have had about him. Something that may hint at this betrayal Mrs. Abernathy was talking about. Also, call the Barlowe Hotel and see if they even have room service. If you can manage it, see if Portia and Beau were there all afternoon on Friday."

"I'll stay here with Jane. I'm quite good on the phone, myself," Benny said.

"Only if you behave," Pen said with a warning tone.

Benny gave her a saucy salute, then settled comfortably behind her desk.

She left with Richard, who drove them to Aristotle's Book Dealer first. Taylor Comeau was still limping from the back when he heard the bell above the door.

"You're back," he said with a frown, he noted she wasn't carrying the first edition she'd claimed she had last time.

"This is Detective Richard Prescott, Mr. Comeau," Penelope announced, gauging his reaction.

His eyes widened with alarm, which gave her the satisfaction she was on the right track. He quickly smoothed his features and gave them a considering look.

"Is that meant to intimidate me?"

"I know for a fact you were undervaluing Mrs. Abernathy's books. I have proof that she planned on publicizing it and exposing you as a fraud," she lied.

Instead of another look of alarm, he seemed confused. "Why would she have done that?"

"Why would she have exposed you as someone who cheated unsuspecting widows?" Pen asked, incredulous.

"Yes, I thought we had an understanding."

"What understanding was that?" Richard asked.

"She didn't care about me undervaluing her husband's books. Hell, I think she would have given them to me, so long as I brought her all the silly romance novels and art books she wanted." He gave them a lofty look. "Honestly, it was an affront to my love of proper literature and the artistry of a properly bound book. These new paperbacks gaining popularity will be the ruin of the book world. But the volumes she brought me were...spectacular. All of them were beautifully maintained, as though they'd never been read."

Penelope pondered that for a brief minute. Spencer Abernathy really had been all show and no substance. He hadn't even read those glorious tomes he had collected.

"I find this very hard to believe," Pen said.

"Believe what you want. Dorothy despised her late husband. I suspect part of the enjoyment came from me undervaluing them, knowing how much he would have hated that. She was happy to be rid of them, and I was happy to oblige. It wasn't as though she needed the money."

That much was true.

"So no, I didn't kill her. In fact, and I know it's going to sound insensitive, I'm particularly saddened she's dead for business and personal reasons." He sighed heavily, ignoring the looks of disdain cast his way. "When I think of all the volumes she still has left, just sitting there exposed to the sun. Heaven knows, that horrid maid of hers didn't dust them nearly enough." He sighed heavily again, closing his eyes in lament.

"So you've been to her apartment?"

His eyes flashed open. "I'm sorry?"

"How do you know the books are exposed to the sun? Or that the maid didn't dust them enough?"

His eyes narrowed slightly, as though wondering if answering honestly would catch him in some sort of trap. It only made him all the more suspicious in Penelope's eyes.

"Zounds!" She said with impatience before strutting over and reaching around to smack the back of his right thigh as hard as she could.

The sound he made could have put a wolf's howl to

shame. Mr. Comeau fell against the bookcase, grabbing the back of his thigh in pain.

Pen gasped in surprise and outrage. She hadn't expected a reaction, she just wanted a shortcut to eliminating him as the man who had attacked her.

"It was *you* that night!"

Richard was instantly by her side, menacingly leaning over Taylor. "Did you attack Miss Banks two nights ago?"

"W-what? No! I...I was, er—"

"Where were you Monday night?" Richard demanded in a voice that had Taylor momentarily mute. Pen feared he might physically attack the man, even though the thought of that gave her a slight thrill.

"I...I didn't mean to attack you!" Taylor finally blurted out.

Richard and Penelope reeled back at the confession that had come so quickly.

He continued, babbling the rest out. "I thought you were her maid. In the dark and bundled up like that you looked similar. Not that that's any better, I know, but I just wanted the dogs. I stumbled and fell into you, knocking you over. You were struggling so much and screaming and I just wanted to silence you and take the dogs, that's all! Then that damn dog bit me and it didn't seem worth it. I wasn't going to hurt you, I just...I've always been clumsy."

All the outrage and anger and fear that had been brewing in Penelope since it happened evaporated, or at least faded somewhat. Putting a face and name to the attacker, realizing it was just some silly little book dealer and not a crazed lunatic, helped.

"But why? What did you want with Dot and Dash?"

"I didn't want them, I just wanted them out of the way, at least for a little while."

"Why?" Richard demanded.

Mr. Comeau seemed to realize he had every reason to remain quiet. "I-I think I'll invoke my right to silence now."

"Oh, no you don't!" Penelope said, her outrage bubbling to the surface again. "I want a reason!"

"And I have rights." Taylor lifted his chin defiantly.

It was Penelope's turn to lean in menacingly. "If you think I'm going to let it go at that, you're very mistaken. You're already going to be charged. I can make those charges far worse than they otherwise would be."

"What?" His eyes widened with alarm.

"Your hands were all over me, grabbing and tearing at my clothes, reaching to wrap around my neck even."

"That's not true!"

"Who's to say? Only the dogs were our witnesses. I know whose side the jury will take. Otherwise, it's your word against mine, a woman who has a very close relationship with a highly decorated detective." Pen didn't feel bad about this bit of blackmail. The attack still haunted her, and Mr. Comeau could claim he had fallen all he wanted. She certainly didn't remember it that way. At the very least, he'd stalked her, waiting until she was all alone and vulnerable in the dark.

Taylor gawped, his eyes wide with fear and outrage. Pen got the satisfaction that he had some idea of what she had felt that night.

"Fine, I suppose it doesn't matter since I wasn't successful." He worked his jaw and pushed himself up higher against the bookcase, glaring at both of them. "Yes, I'd been in her apartment before. I was invited, mind you! In retrospect, I realize it was her way of showing me just how much she had to offer. She would dangle each volume like a carrot, for more and more in return. A *first* edition of *Moby*

Dick? In *mint* condition? Even some of the more recent ones like *Call of the Wild.* Frankly, it would have been easier just to pay the fair value and be done with it all!

"Then, when I'd heard in the evening papers Monday night that she had been murdered, all I could think about was those volumes going to some idiot relative who would probably donate them to a charity bin or use them as bedtime reading material for their sniveling children. I had to have them!

"I knew the staff had their own quarters they retired to at night. I was also familiar with the service entrance that had no pesky doorman standing watch. All I had to do was get in and...take them. The only problem would have been the dogs, alerting anyone to my presence. I thought it would be easy to just get a hold of the leashes when they were taken out for their late walk—Dorothy had told me their schedule—lose them somewhere in the city for a while, until I got what I wanted. That's it!"

"That's it?" Pen said with a laugh. "That's certainly enough, don't you think?"

"I never went through with any of it though, did I? Well, except for the part with you." He at least had the good grace to look sorry.

"Did you have a key to get into the building and apartment?" Richard asked.

"No, I planned on picking the locks. By now, I've become an expert at it." He quickly added, "Out of occupational necessity! Do you have any idea how many tomes left by the deceased are locked away in chests and cabinets, even safes, all with loved ones who have no idea where the keys are? That would have been the easiest obstacle. It was the dogs I was most worried about."

"Your first plan didn't work so you decided to attack me to get the dogs out of the way?" Penelope probed.

"What first plan? That idiotic attack was my only attempt."

"You're going to have to tell us where you were Friday, all day."

"I was with potential clients. Two siblings whose father had just died, leaving the most wonderful library. This field is rife with vultures, some of whom *would* probably commit murder to get their hands on a valuable collection. I didn't tell you before because I was worried about it getting out and being cheated out of it. Who knows what loose lips you and the police might have?"

Pen gave him an incredulous look.

"I'll give you their information, they live in Connecticut. Check with them! I was there from noon until dinnertime. I couldn't have killed Dorothy."

Or brought the flowers that almost killed Dot and Dash.

"Alright, Mr. Comeau, I'm arresting you for assault...to start."

"What? But I told you—"

"You still attacked me!" Pen spat.

He pouted like a petulant child, as though he'd done no more than steal a cookie from a jar. Richard put him in handcuffs and used his phone to call for uniformed officers to take him to the station. After that, he came back to join Penelope while Taylor sulked in a chair.

"Highly decorated detective?" Richard murmured with a grin.

"Well, you should be at any rate."

"I suppose this solves at least one mystery. I'll check with the family he mentioned. If he was there then he didn't kill Mrs. Abernathy or bring the flowers. Which means he may not have stolen the jewelry either."

"No, I suspect that man only finds value in books, anyway," she said with a sigh. "At least I don't have to bring Dot and Dash along anymore."

"So we're still in search of a murderer and a jewelry thief. I assume you haven't heard back from your source who shall not be named about the necklace? You'll have to update him on the additional pieces that were stolen."

"He'll be the one to get in touch with me," she said. She was beginning to regret having gone through Tommy and Mr. Sweeney. They would eventually come back to her for their pound of flesh in return. Their methods made Pen's blackmail against Taylor seem like child's play. "Speaking of stolen pieces, I think it's time for a visit to the Lachapelle shop. I have an idea."

CHAPTER TWENTY-SEVEN

R ichard drove Penelope to Percy Dawson's shop. They didn't have an appointment, but she figured with a detective at her side, Percy would have to make an exception.

Before they even reached the door, Pen could see that something about the shop had changed. There were fewer pieces on display through the windows. Inside, Percy was beaming as he showed a piece to a customer. Looking past her, he saw Richard and Penelope approaching and his eyes widened with alarm. He glared and subtly shook his head, trying to ward them off.

Richard simply pulled out his badge and placed it against the window. It made a soft tinkling sound that might as well have been the roar of a lion for how much it made Percy flinch. It became obvious they weren't leaving until he opened the door. Penelope saw him give a sigh, hold up one finger to his customer, and then rush over to them.

He opened the door just a crack and hissed in a low voice, "As you can see I'm with a customer. You can make an appointment and come back. Unless of course you have a warrant?"

"No but we do have some pertinent questions," Penelope said.

His eyes turned to slits. "Well then, I repeat, you can come back when—"

"We know it was you selling the fakes as real Lachapelle pieces several years ago." She may have used a louder voice than necessary, but it had its intended effect.

Percy instantly opened the door and rushed outside, despite wearing no coat for the freezing temperature. He slammed the door closed behind him. "Are you deliberately trying to scare off my customer? Is that how the police operate now?" He turned to glare at Richard.

"We're *trying* to find a murderer," Richard replied in a harsh voice.

"We have proof, or rather Dorothy Abernathy had proof it was you. Is that why she was upset with you? Did she threaten you? Is that why you killed her?"

"Killed her? What the hell are you talking about? I wasn't anywhere near her Friday, as I already stated."

"But it *was* you selling the replicas, was it not? Don't try and deny it."

"You have no proof, otherwise you would have given it. As for Mrs. Abernathy's murder, you have even less proof of that."

An interesting denial, Penelope thought. She'd been suspicious of his having been responsible for the fake pieces, and he had just hinted there might be some truth to that. As for the murder, she still couldn't tell.

"If you won't give an alibi, I can only assume you had means and opportunity."

"You can't arrest me based on that!" Percy didn't look certain of the fact, though Pen knew he was right.

"Perhaps, but I *can* keep returning here, disrupting your business, questioning your customers until one of them gives you an alibi." He arched an eyebrow.

The blood drained from Percy's face, or perhaps the cold was finally getting to him. "Fine! I was...at the bank. Piedmont Savings & Loan."

"All afternoon?" Pen asked, incredulous.

"From one until two."

"That still leaves—"

"And then from two until almost four-thirty, I was at North Manhattan Trust, another bank. You're welcome to check with both."

"Two banks, and for that long? What could you have possibly been doing?"

"What I was doing was my business, certainly not yours," he scoffed.

"He was securing a loan," Richard said, sounding resigned.

"A loan? What for?" Pen blurted out in frustration.

"Again, my business, not yours," Percy snapped, looking worried He glanced back into the store as though hoping his client hadn't heard.

Penelope's eyes followed his into the shop, where his customer looked on with a mixture of concern and curiosity. She scanned the shelves, realizing what it was that was different about the shop.

"Zounds! You were using the loan to buy up your own merchandise!"

"What?" Percy blurted out.

"Yes, that's it! You're artificially fixing the market on

Lachapelle figurines in your own store." Thanks to her father she knew something about market manipulation. She coughed out a sharp laugh, as she eyed the customer. "Did you send out a notice to all your valued customers that certain pieces were forever gone? That they'd better hurry and make an appointment before even more flew from the shelves?"

The blood that had left his face earlier came rushing back, turning to flames of embarrassment across his cheeks and forehead.

"There's no law against that." Again, he sounded uncertain, even darting his eyes to Detective Prescott for reassurance.

"No, but I'm sure Lachapelle wouldn't look too kindly on it. They might decide you aren't the proper distributor on the East Coast for their merchandise. I wonder if the bank that finally gave you the loan knows what its actual intended purpose was?"

"What do you want from me? I didn't kill her! You have your answer as to where I was."

"We do," Richard said in resignation. He gave Percy a hard look. "And I *will* be checking with those banks."

"Do it! Just leave me alone." Percy glared at both of them, then opened the door and went back into the shop. He made a point of locking the door behind him, giving them another hard glare before returning to his customer.

"If he was at the banks for that long, he wasn't the one to lure Mrs. Abernathy into the park. And the flowers were already at the apartment when Sally returned for the dog food."

"So we've narrowed the murderer down to two men."

"The problem is, Taylor and Percy were the two most likely suspects as far as doing something that would make Mrs. Abernathy feel cheated. At least anything obvious.

With Beau and Alan, there's nothing that I can think of, at least not enough to commit murder over. It's quite obvious Beau wasn't faithful only to her. Still, I doubt she would have expected that from him. As for Alan, well, Benny assured me he was one of his ilk, but I'd like to think she would have been understanding about that, rather than try to expose him for it."

"Perhaps it's something else entirely."

"It would have had to be something she recently discovered, something that would have had either Alan or Beau rushing to plead their case on Friday." Pen searched her memory, reviewing everything she'd seen or learned about Mrs. Abernathy.

"I've got it!" She said suddenly. "I know where to go next."

CHAPTER TWENTY-EIGHT

R ichard was driving as Penelope sat animatedly talking next to him. "It was in the receipts Alice and I went through. I didn't think anything of it as it seemed like an ordinary expenditure someone of Mrs. Abernathy's stature might have. Now, especially considering the timeline, it makes sense. At least I hope so."

They arrived at the address Penelope remembered from the receipt she'd seen from Mrs. Abernathy's desk. Lyons of New York was situated in an elegant office that took up two floors on 6th Avenue, right on the edge of Ladies' Mile, where many of the nicer department stores were located.

The offices opened up to a floor that looked like a combination bank and museum. There were several perfectly ordered desks for clerks to attend to their business. However, the space was strategically dotted with unique items that were obviously quite valuable: vases, statues, masterpiece oils, and elaborate jewelry encased in glass boxes.

A pretty receptionist planted a smile on her face as they

entered. "Hello, welcome to Lyons of New York, how can we be of service?"

Richard discreetly revealed his badge, causing only the slightest flutter of her eyelashes. "We would like to speak to the individual who worked with Mrs. Dorothy Abernathy recently?"

Her smile brightened, though it now seemed artificial. "One moment, let me call Mr. Ezring. He can assist you."

Penelope and Richard waited as she quietly called him on an internal line and explained the situation. When she hung up, the artificially large smile was back on. "He'll be with you in just a moment. In the meantime, can I get you coffee or tea?"

Richard and Pen both declined. One moment later, a very short, slightly round man approached, with a pleasantly open expression on his face. He was impeccably dressed in a well-tailored, three-piece black suit with the barest hint of pinstripes.

"I'm Stafford Ezring, why don't you come into my office so we can speak privately."

They followed him into an office at the back of the open area. He closed the door and also offered them something to drink, to which they again declined.

"I understand you are here about Mrs. Abernathy?"

"Yes, I'm Detective Richard Prescott and this is Miss Penelope Banks, who is assisting me."

Pen decided it was best to let Richard take the lead in that instance, as it was an official visit. They were far more likely to get answers under the impression he'd given.

"A terrible thing that happened, I read of it in the newspaper," Mr. Ezring shook his head ruefully.

"Yes, I assume she came here to get something

appraised. I'd like to know what it was, as it may help in my investigation."

Mr. Ezring paused before answering. "Usually we are quite strict about client confidentiality. Under normal circumstances, I would request a warrant or subpoena. However, I can see that this is a special case, and of course, we at Lyons want to assist the police whenever possible. As such, yes, Mrs. Abernathy came in to have her jewelry appraised, as she planned to sell all of it. That is another service we provide as well, of course."

"Just the jewelry? And she wanted to sell *all* of it?" Richard confirmed.

Jacob Millington had claimed as much, which lent even more credence to his confessions about their relationship.

"Yes." Mr. Ezring took a small breath before continuing. "Unfortunately, several pieces in her collection were paste."

"*Fakes?*" Pen exclaimed

Mr. Ezring nodded solemnly. "Obviously, she was quite upset over the discovery."

"So her husband had given her fake jewelry?" Penelope asked, incredulous at the audacity of the man.

Mr. Ezring gave Penelope only the barest look of disapproval, no doubt wondering why she was so boldly asking questions. "Oh no, Mrs. Abernathy had been a customer with us before. We had appraised all her jewelry in the past, the last time was just after her husband had died, I believe. Each piece was perfectly authentic at the time."

"So in between then and now, someone had replaced the jewelry with paste without her knowledge," Richard confirmed.

"So it would seem."

"Did she give any indication as to whom she thought might have done it?" Richard asked.

"Not that I'm aware of. I think she was simply more surprised than anything. Part of our service includes private investigation for cases of theft and fraud, but she declined. She seemed embarrassed over the whole affair. I tried to reassure her that someone taking advantage of her that way was no taint on her. She certainly wouldn't have been the first widow to be taken advantage of in such a way. More than anything she would be pitied."

Which was the worst thing he could have possibly said, Pen thought.

"I assume there was an account of exactly which pieces were paste and which were real? If so, I'll be needing that list."

"Of course, as I stated, anything we can do to help the police."

"Was the diamond and sapphire necklace paste?" Pen asked.

"Fortunately, that was still very real. A good thing, as it was her most expensive piece. It was probably so intricate, it would have taken longer to reproduce. As it was, I put her in touch with a buyer who would be interested in purchasing it from her. Despite everything, she made a small joke about wearing it all the time for safekeeping. Also, just to remember what it felt like to wear real jewels before she sold them off."

And perhaps it had gotten her killed.

"Just to be clear, she gave you no information that might indicate who replaced her jewelry, or how and when it may have been stolen?"

"I'm afraid not. You don't suppose that was the cause of her murder, do you?" He looked concerned, no doubt wondering how it might affect his firm.

Richard tactfully evaded the question. "Thank you for

your time, Mr. Ezring. If I could have a copy of that list of fakes and genuine pieces?"

A small pout of disappointment came to his mouth. "Yes, of course. I'll have my secretary create a copy for you. If there's nothing else?"

"No, again thank you for your time."

Richard and Penelope rose to leave. After collecting the list of jewelry, both real and fake, from Mr. Ezring's secretary, they left. Outside, it had started to snow heavily.

"Well, this should make this investigation that much easier," Richard said as they hurried back to his car.

"So it was jewelry that she was upset about," Penelope said. "It has to be Beau, I'd say."

"How do you figure that?" Richard said, not in an argumentative tone, but in a way that encouraged her to think out loud.

"He strongly suggested Mrs. Abernathy's relationship with him was quite intimate. If so, he must have visited her apartment at least once. Maybe to drop off the paintings even. Out of all four men, she may have even trusted him enough to give him his own key!"

"Go on," Richard urged.

"He would assume someone like Mrs. Abernathy would have had expensive jewelry. Perhaps he'd even done a little wandering out of curiosity while he was there. Who wouldn't, with all that luxury on display? He found the jewelry and studied it enough to create replicas. Or perhaps he stole it, had the fakes made, and replaced them on a subsequent visit."

"That's a lot of supposition. Plus, he has an alibi for Friday, doesn't he?"

"From some silly little girl who's goofy for him. I think she'd say anything to defend him. That alibi shouldn't be hard to break. Who could possibly keep tabs on them all afternoon at that hotel, well into five o'clock? And it isn't all that far from the Alstonian. Plenty of time for him to lure Mrs. Abernathy into the park with whatever charm he worked on her in the first place, strangle her, and steal the necklace, which he would know wasn't fake."

"And the flowers in her apartment? The rest of the jewelry that was stolen? Did he make a subsequent visit for that?"

Pen considered it. Killing Mrs. Abernathy and then taking the time to get the flowers, come back, break-in, and steal the jewelry? It didn't seem likely. Unless Portia had been completely lying about being with him at all that afternoon.

"For the amount those remaining jewels were worth, I think he'd risk it. More importantly, he'd want to search for and get rid of any proof she may have had. To avoid a prison sentence, I think he'd definitely attempt it. Maybe he gave Portia something so she'd fall asleep for hours?"

"You have a point about motive. Avoiding prison while at the same time reaping a nice little windfall in jewels? Yes, I'd make the time to do all that as well."

"Good to know in case you ever think of stealing my jewels and killing my pets."

Richard gave her a sardonic look.

Pen laughed softly. "We'll see what Jane discovered about him. I've suspected from the start he isn't all he seems."

"Don't get ahead of yourself, my dear."

"When do I ever?"

"Should I answer that?" Richard responded with a laugh.

Back at the office, the two buzzing little worker bees had indeed been quite busy. After Pen detailed that morning's adventures—they were quite amused at how she'd exposed Taylor Comeau as her attacker—it was their turn to relay what they had learned.

Jane was the overly excited one to speak first. "Beau Blackman is *not* a full-time teacher at the school! He's only filling in for a teacher who is away on some sabbatical. He has no permanent position there, nor is there one waiting for him."

Penelope gave Richard a satisfied smile. "Well, so much for his being so casually dismissive of Mrs. Abernathy's offer. Not that there was one in the first place. Without a position at the school, he probably wanted nothing more than to travel first class to Europe with someone else paying the way. Perhaps he approached her Friday in the hopes that she would change her mind and take him instead. Maybe when she said no, he thought the necklace would suffice as a substitute and he ended up strangling her in the process of taking it. At the very least, we have something to question him with."

"About that..." Benny said, clearing his throat just to fully capture everyone's attention. "I made a little phone call to the Barlowe Hotel."

"And?" Pen asked, feeling her disappointment set in preemptively.

"They did confirm that several people saw him in the room with Portia Friday afternoon."

"How'd you manage to get that information?" Pen knew such hotels were quite protective of their guests' privacy.

"I have my methods. Suffice it to say, they were on the seventh floor, in case you need confirmation."

"And they can confirm he was there from noon until at least five?"

"Well...no. They delivered room service at one, then again at four. He was quite memorable, of course. Surely that puts a bit of doubt in the idea it was Beau, who murdered her? Didn't you tell us your doorman said she left around three?"

"If I didn't know any better I'd say you were happy about that."

"I hate to see such a beautiful man wasting away in prison," Benny said, plumping out his bottom lip.

"Perhaps that beautiful man shouldn't have committed a crime."

"We don't know for a fact he did."

"Fine, we'll plot it out like a proper investigation."

"I'll get the chalkboard!" Jane said, jumping up to get it.

"We need two columns, one for Alan Lashbrook and one for Beau Blackman. The other two can be eliminated, as they presumably have solid alibis."

Jane created the columns.

"Let's start with Alan, just to get him out of the way."

"Or uncover him as the killer," Richard countered.

"Yes, yes," Pen said, waving a hand dismissively. "Firstly, he said he was allergic to dogs. Thus, he wouldn't have spent any time with dogs, certainly not enough to know what flowers might harm them."

"He *claimed* he was allergic to dogs, and it isn't difficult to find out what flowers might kill them," Richard said. "Mrs. Abernathy may have even told him at some point."

Jane stood with the chalk in the air over the board, wondering which statement to put down.

Pen frowned at Richard. "He was at the club that after-noon, as I've told you."

Richard arched an eyebrow. "And even you confessed that wasn't an ironclad alibi."

Pen turned to face him, hands on her hips. "He has plenty of wealthy women from whom to feather his nest. He'd hardly be upset by losing the patronage of one. And their relationship couldn't have been anything more than strictly companions."

Richard faced her, arms crossed over his chest. "*Unless* he implied otherwise, only for her to find out the truth and be upset about it. If she threatened to tell all the other women he taught, that would certainly create motive."

"Why do you refuse to consider it may be Beau?"

"Why do you refuse to consider it may be Alan?"

"I don't, I just think it's far more likely that Beau had a reason to be resentful and need the money."

"It seems to me, he had already replaced her with someone else."

"With a young woman who will soon enough wake up to the reality that her parents would never approve of such a match, and marry her off to a more suitable man."

"Now there, you have a sensible response that creates motive."

Pen blinked, surprised Richard had finally been swayed.

"Oh, don't stop now!" Benny drawled. "The tension between you two is positively the cat's meow."

Penelope narrowed her eyes at Richard, still heated over their exchange. "Are you just appeasing me so we'll stop arguing? You should know by now that I'm not some spoiled princess who needs coddling that way."

"And you should know by now I would never coddle you. Arguing things out this way is good for—"

"Pineapples!"

Benny chuckled. "I wouldn't have thought arguing would be good for that, but I'm willing to be educated."

Penelope turned to give him a smirk. "Princess."

"I beg your pardon?" Benny said, pressing a hand to his chest with mock offense as though she were calling him a name.

"Your friend from the club. He said something about the women to whom Alan gave lessons wanting to do the waltz and feel like a princess." Pen nibbled on her thumb and paced. "The woman we saw coming from his class that day, she was wearing quite a bit of jewelry."

"She was. Rather gaudy, if you ask me," Benny said in agreement.

"I've done the Charleston and the Black Bottom Stomp. Even the foxtrot would be rather cumbersome with that amount of jewelry on."

"So he must have had them remove it," Jane said, catching on quickly.

"Perhaps he had them put into a safe or some kind of locked cabinet."

"The kind with a false back," Richard said. "It's a classic con. The women deposit their jewelry during class. Meanwhile, someone else comes and takes it—"

"Like his assistant, Clarice!" Jane said.

"Right," Pen agreed. "At first, just to inspect it, maybe take a photograph or sketch it out so someone can create an exact replica. Then, the next time she wears it, they simply replace it with the fake jewelry."

"My, my, he is rather the devious sort."

"It makes so much sense," Penelope said, then gasped.

"Pineapples! That day I saw Mrs. Abernathy wearing her jewelry, it was a Thursday, the same day she took her dance lessons! I can't believe I didn't consider that sooner."

"Don't beat yourself up over it, Penelope. Your mind can't always perform perfectly. Besides, three days is a good run for solving a murder case."

She twisted her lips. "We still have to prove it."

"I'm fine with the Penelope Banks style of getting a confession, simply confronting him—minus the attack with a purse, of course."

"That was a rare and exceptional circumstance, which worked, mind you. So, Detective Prescott, what are we waiting for? Let's go nab our murder suspect."

CHAPTER TWENTY-NINE

On the drive to the Lashbrook Dance Studio, Richard and Penelope devised a plan for collecting evidence and getting Alan to confess. Pen would pretend to be interested in taking classes, and get him to give a tour, where she'd search for the place where clients kept their jewelry during lessons. Richard would obviously not come inside with her. She had brought Jane along to help, should things have gotten perilous and she needed to flag down Richard for help. Benny insisted on going, claiming he had participated enough to see things through. They agreed, so long as he stayed in the car with Detective Prescott.

After one quick stop, Richard dropped Jane and Penelope at the corner and they walked to the studio. When Clarice opened the door, she instantly glared and began shutting it in their face.

"Wait, please! I have an update about Mrs. Abernathy's case. We know Mr. Lashbrook is innocent. I owe you an apology."

That at least got her to pause. She peered at them, still with suspicion in her gaze. "What do you want?"

"As I stated, I came to formally apologize, and also to inquire about taking dance lessons from Mr. Lashbrook."

Her gaze softened. The way Penelope's coat just happened to drape open slightly, revealing the cheap but convincing costume jewelry they had purchased on the way there, certainly helped. Penelope had never developed a fondness for expensive jewelry the way some women did, especially the kind that sparkled enough to draw attention, so they'd had to improvise. Blessedly, Clarice's eyes lingered on the sparkling piece around her neck.

"Please do come in." She opened the door wider for them.

Pen exhaled with relief as she and Jane entered.

"Mr. Lashbrook is with a student now, I'm afraid, but he should be done soon. You said you had an update on the case?"

"Yes, but I should probably tell him myself, as part of my formal apology. I'm sure he'll be relieved to know he's no longer under any suspicion."

"Yes, I'm sure," she said, a professional smile plastered on her face. "Would you like a cup of coffee or tea to warm you up? It's so blistery outside!"

"It is," Pen agreed. She noted that there was no coffee or tea service visible, which meant that the assistant would have to go into a back office to make it. "Yes, I would love some coffee, with two spoonfuls of sugar, and Jane likes tea, with milk if you have it. If it isn't too much trouble of course." The additives should at least add a few seconds to how long she remained in the back.

"Not at all." She gave a perfunctory smile and left them.

They now had the waiting area to themselves. Penelope quickly shot up and rushed to the desk. She quietly pulled open drawers, rifling through office supplies and papers, committing everything she saw to memory. The only surprising thing she found was a gun. Perhaps it was for safety?

Pen left it, and turned to the file cabinet. She opened the top drawer and saw files, each labeled with a woman's name, presumably all of Alan's students. As much as she would have liked to open just one of them, she heard the assistant coming back. Pen hissed to herself and quietly closed the drawer before returning to her seat just in time. She had seen nothing incriminating, not that she expected to find concrete evidence of an ongoing jewelry theft just lying there in a file cabinet. If it was as sophisticated as it seemed, they wouldn't have been that dumb.

"Thank you," she said, accepting the coffee.

"Thank you," Jane echoed, accepting her tea.

"Why don't I get started on the paperwork while I wait?" Penelope figured there might be some helpful information uncovered during the process of becoming a student.

"Mr. Lashbrook likes to conduct the initial interview personally to see if any potential student is a proper fit."

Of course he did. He would have to make sure that his future victims were not only wealthy but owned expensive jewelry as well.

They continued to sip their drinks and wait patiently. Penelope studied the waiting area but found nothing suspicious. Whatever scheme was going on, it certainly wouldn't have been out in the open like that.

They heard the door to the studio open, and next to her, Jane jumped a bit. Pen maintained a calm facade.

Alan escorted an older woman out of his studio. Her jewelry wasn't nearly as ostentatious as the first woman's, but it looked expensive enough. When he saw Penelope and Jane in the waiting area, he gave them the same glare of suspicion his assistant first had. He waited until his client had left to turn on them.

"What are you doing here? I've said all I have to say to you."

"She's here to apologize," Clarice said.

"Yes, it seems I was wrong about you being a suspect with regard to Mrs. Abernathy. The police are looking at someone else for her murder. I wanted to come and apologize to you personally."

He calmed down, clearing his throat and smoothing a hand over his front. "Yes, well, it was quite the disruption. Reputation is everything in my business. Just the hint of suspicion would be enough to ruin me."

"Which is why I also wanted to apply to take lessons with you. If Mrs. Abernathy enjoyed them, then you must be quite good at what you do. She did love dancing, and so do I."

He considered her with a degree of skepticism. She noted the way his eyes landed on her jewelry. If he suspected it was bait, he didn't show it. In fact, his eyes lit up just as his assistant's had.

"I suppose I can indulge a brief inquiry. I should let you know, I don't limit myself to one form of dance. If you're looking to focus only on the sorts of dances you'd find in today's clubs, you'll be disappointed. I try to create a well-rounded experience for my dance partners, exposing them to the entire world of dance."

"Perfect," Penelope exclaimed, as though that was exactly what she was hoping for.

"Well then, as it turns out, my afternoon is free. Why

don't you come with me and we can discuss it while I give you a tour?"

It was going perfectly. Pen rose and followed Alan, leaving Jane to finish her tea and keep watch in the waiting area.

"As I stated, I open my students up to all forms of dance. Some come wanting only to learn the waltz or tango. I have a broader view of things. I insist that they dedicate at least some portion of each lesson to modern dance."

"Like the Charleston?" Pen asked innocently.

"Exactly."

He led her into the studio, which presented quite the surprise. It didn't look like any studio she'd seen. It looked like a small ballroom. There was a chandelier above, and scrolled molding on all the walls, save for one appropriately lined with a mirror.

"I can tell you are surprised," he said proudly. "I like to immerse my students in the experience. This room is reserved for waltz and other classic ballroom dances. I even encourage my students to dress the part. Why not play Cinderella going to the ball?"

"Like a princess," Pen said with a smile.

"Exactly. Just one of the many things that distinguish me from other instructors. The second studio is of course more traditional, where the focus is on form and movement."

"You mentioned teaching various forms of dance per session? I assume that means I'd have to change at some point?"

"Yes, we have a private changing area. I'll show you."

Pen followed him into a dressing room that was just as glamorous as the ballroom. It might have been a dressing room in a New York mansion or luxury apartment.

"You mentioned a princess, and that is exactly what I aim for."

"Should I bring my tiara?" Pen said teasingly.

"Why not?" He said with a broad smile, as though that was not only acceptable, but preferred. "I have several clients who do in fact bring tiaras to wear. Your finest clothes and jewelry shouldn't be left for grand affairs that happen only once in a blue moon. Just because it's a private lesson, doesn't mean you shouldn't dress the part."

"Surely I wouldn't be dancing the Charleston in a tiara?"

He gave an indulgent laugh. "No, no, of course not. We have a safe where you can place your valuables until the lesson is over."

"An actual safe? My, you do provide every service." Pen looked around. "Where is it?"

"Come with me." He led her down a hallway and took hold of the frame of a painting. It was a secret door that opened to a wall safe. Pen noted that the back of it would have abutted the back room behind Clarice's desk.

She had him.

"Well, this all sounds wonderful. How does one sign up?"

He brightened, his eyes inadvertently falling to her fake necklace. "I'll have Clarice get you started with the paperwork."

He led her back to the front area, telling her more about the lessons, including the absurd cost. The women he catered to really must have been lonely *and* wealthy. Shame on him for taking advantage of them twice over.

"Hmm, at that price, I really do need to consider it."

Alan blinked, his gaze darting down to her necklace and

back again in confusion. "One really can't put a price tag on experience, Miss Banks."

Pen tilted her head, studying him in a new light now that she was certain he was the murderer. She should have waited for Jane to leave and get Richard but she couldn't help herself.

"When did Mrs. Abernathy confront you about her stolen jewelry?"

"I beg your pardon?" Alan said, at first looking bewildered.

"That is why you approached her Friday, isn't it? She figured out it was you who had been replacing her real jewels with paste, no?"

Sudden realization hit his eyes.

"It's a trick, Alan!" Clarice exclaimed, confirming that she was working with him.

"Shut up, Clarice," he hissed. His gaze suddenly narrowed. "Stop them before they—"

"I don't think so," Pen said, reaching into her purse and pulling out her small gun with a jade handle. She stepped back so that both of them were in her line of sight. She saw that Clarice had opened the drawer with the gun, but hadn't had a chance to grab it. "Move away from the desk, miss."

She saw the assistant consider going for the gun. "Don't do it. I'll shoot before you can pull it out," Pen bluffed. "Is he really worth dying for?"

Clarice exhaled and wisely stepped away.

"Jane, please get Detective Prescott." She heard Jane quickly leave behind her.

Alan's eyes widened, then turned to slits. He grinned with satisfaction. "You have no proof of anything!"

"I have that safe you just showed me. I'm guessing there's a false back to it that Clarice here has access to?"

"Even if so, that proves nothing. That's not even enough for probable cause." He grinned.

"Mary Shepsman. Sarah Washer. Marilyn Sherry." Pen continued reciting the names from the file folders she had glanced at during her quick scan of the cabinet contents. Alan's sneer faded with each one.

Penelope heard the door open and close behind her. Richard rushed to her side, his gun already drawn as well.

"Well done, Annie Oakley," she heard Benny croon with a soft laugh.

"Are you alright? He didn't hurt you did he?" Richard asked.

"Not at all. In fact, I was just reminding Mr. Lashbrook here about all the other clients who should probably go and have their jewelry appraised, particularly those pieces he encouraged them to wear for their, ah, immersive dance experiences. He had them place them into a safe during the *mandatory* modern dance lessons."

"You saw it?"

"I saw it," Pen confirmed. "You'll find the fake back somewhere in Clarice's office."

"Which provides motive," Richard said.

"I'll bet we won't find anyone who saw you actually using the gym at your club on Friday, will we?"

Alan's face went white. Pen wasn't sure if it was due to the fact that she knew about his private club, or that she had confirmed that he wouldn't have an alibi at the time of the murder.

"I had nothing to do with the murder, I swear! That was all him!" Clarice shouted.

"Shut up, you stupid woman!" Alan snapped. It was

only Richard intervening that kept him from lunging at his assistant.

"But why try to kill the dogs?" Pen asked, now that the murder was confirmed and Richard had him in a hold.

"What?" Alan looked truly surprised, enough to stop struggling in Richard's grip.

"Friday, you brought lavender and hydrangeas to Mrs. Abernathy's apartment and fed it to her dogs when you went to steal her jewelry. Was that just out of spite?"

"I've never even been to her apartment. Why would I feed flowers to dogs? Are you accusing me of trying to kill them as well? That doesn't make any sense. I told you, I was allergic. You're not putting that on me!"

Pen blinked in surprise. She met Richard's eyes, and he seemed just as confounded.

It seemed they had one more arrest to make.

CHAPTER THIRTY

Richard and Penelope went to the art school alone. Benny hadn't been aware of just how tedious and involved it was to finalize an arrest for murder. They'd had to wait for the uniformed police to arrive and take Alan and Clarice away, then get statements, and cordon everything off. By the time all was said and done, hours later, he was bored of it all and decided to return to his life of idle pleasure.

There would always be some party they'd end up at together to reunite and perhaps reminisce.

Penelope certainly wasn't going to expose Jane to any more danger. She figured Alfred would probably disinvite her to the wedding if his fiancée had to face another situation with guns.

The two remaining investigators on the case were pleased to learn that Beau was at the school. They found him in an empty classroom, working on an oil painting of a marble bust. His paintbrush paused when he saw the two of them enter.

"No Portia by your side today?" Penelope observed.

A crooked grin came to his face and he returned to his painting. "She isn't surgically attached to me, Miss Banks. Besides, we have decided to go our separate ways. It's for the best. The school would have frowned on the relationship."

"Or perhaps she realized that she was hitching her wagon to a possible murderer?"

His eyes slid to Penelope, and that crooked smile came back. "I didn't kill Dorothy."

"I wasn't talking about her."

Once again he paused, this time only briefly. Then, he laughed. "And who is it I supposedly killed now?"

"Dot and Dash—when you stole Mrs. Abernathy's jewelry."

He erupted with heavier laughter. "I seem to recall you mentioning they were still quite alive. As for her jewelry, I didn't steal it." He flashed a smirk at her. "I don't think any of it really would have suited me."

"Someone saw you enter the building carrying those flowers on Friday."

"No, they didn't." He sounded almost bored as he went on painting. Of course he would have made sure no one saw him. She didn't bother bringing up the jewelry box, knowing he'd not only deny having disposed of it—the police had in fact found it in the trash area in the basement of the Alstonian—but he would have been smart enough to wear gloves.

Penelope turned to Richard, at a loss. He had left this part to her, as she was usually better at getting people to talk. It was time for him to have a go at it.

"Being that you were such a close friend to Mrs. Abernathy, you'll be happy to know that we did just arrest her murderer." He studied Beau more keenly. "He had been steadily stealing not only her jewelry but that of other women as well, replacing them with paste. In fact, one of the few remaining pieces of Mrs. Abernathy's that was still genuine, she was wearing on her neck that day she was murdered. So whoever stole the rest isn't likely to get any more than one would at a costume shop for paste."

Beau continued painting as though the words rolled right off him, but Pen could see how tight his jaw became, the hard look in his eyes, and the way the brush slashed at the painting with a little more ferocity. It wasn't a confession, certainly not one that would hold up in court, but it was enough for her to know he was guilty.

Pen supposed she would have to be satisfied knowing he now had neither Mrs. Abernathy's patronage nor Portia's. He didn't even have a position teaching painting at—

"'My Petunia,'" she suddenly said.

Beau exhaled slowly, then turned to her with a bemused look. "I beg your pardon?"

"That's what you wrote on the back of one painting I saw. It's interesting, the garden in that painting, out of all the others, had quite a few flowers I would have thought Mrs. Abernathy would have disapproved of."

"Dorothy liked all flowers," he said, sounding slightly disgruntled as he returned to his painting.

"But not always the meaning behind them," Pen said, tilting her head to the side. "I briefly looked through a book on her shelf that explained the meanings behind almost every flower. Petunia meant deep feelings of resentment, anger, and trouble."

"Is that so?" Beau said without looking at her.

"What were you resentful about, Beau? That she was taking someone else to Europe with her? That she was unceremoniously ending whatever relationship she had with you? Had she hinted at promises to take you that she suddenly reneged on? I'll bet that thousand dollars felt like a slap in the face, certainly when compared to a year-long, first-class trip to Europe. Maybe you thought killing or perhaps just harming her beloved dogs would be payback, all while stealing her jewelry?"

Beau sighed and closed his eyes. When he opened them again, there was a hard edge in his gaze as it landed on Penelope. "This is all very fanciful and interesting, Miss Banks. It's also very unprovable."

He was right.

"I suppose so," she said thoughtfully. "I hope you are economical with that parting gift of a thousand dollars. You're going to need it. The rumor mill works differently from a court of law, Mr. Blackman. No one likes men who harm dogs, no matter how handsome and charming they are. In the end, Dot and Dash are fine and healthy. In fact, I'll bet they'll have a better life than you will. I know you haven't been offered a permanent position here at the art school. Your most lucrative patron has been murdered, and the other ended things with you. The jewelry we both know you stole is mostly worthless. All that's left are a few paintings with your name attached that you probably resented creating in the first place."

He was silent, still staring at her with pure rage only barely masked. After a moment he spoke, a slight curl coming to his mouth. "Will that be all?"

Penelope felt her own rage simmer, but she tempered it. "I suppose it is."

Richard interjected. "I should probably make it clear that we have descriptions of every piece of jewelry Mrs. Abernathy owned, complete with the stones. Between the New York Police Department and some rather unsavory people Miss Banks here knows, we *will* be notified if any of it is ever brought in for an appraisal or sold in the black market. As Miss Banks said, I hope you're economical with that thousand dollars."

Penelope and Richard left Beau Blackman, who for once looked perfectly defeated.

"I hate that he might get away with it," Pen seethed once they left the school.

"Get away with what? As you stated, Dot and Dash are fine. The jewelry he stole is either worthless or will be the very evidence that gets him arrested if he ever tries to sell it. I'm sure you'll do your bit to put whispers in a few ears about him poisoning the dogs. I don't see Mr. Blackman having much of a future in decent society, which thus far seems to have been his bread and butter."

That made Penelope feel slightly better. And, after all, they had solved the mystery of Mrs. Abernathy's murder, and the man who had attacked Penelope.

Pen received the message from Tommy the next day. It sounded more like a summons. Thus, that Friday, one week after Dorothy Abernathy had been murdered, she found herself at the Peacock Club, once again in a back room.

This time she was facing Mr. Jack Sweeney himself. Tommy stood behind him, an imposing presence.

"Isn't this a rare treat," she deadpanned, trying to mask the shock of uncertainty running through her veins.

"I thought I would deliver the happy news to you personally. We managed to locate someone who heard a whisper about your necklace. Once he found out yours truly had a vested interest, he was more than happy to introduce himself. It seems he has a longtime connection with a certain someone who has been bringing him jewelry to sell and make replicas of for quite some time now. He gave me a name. Perhaps you'd like to know what it was?"

"No honor among thieves, it seems. Alan Lashbrook?"

He smiled. It was hardly friendly.

"I don't suppose he'd be willing to testify?"

Mr. Sweeney laughed. Which answered that question.

"Come now, Miss Banks, you should have known that much from the start."

"I suppose." Yes, she'd known that from the start. At the time, she had just wanted a name so she could focus her efforts on him. Now that she'd done all the hard work, it hardly seemed worth it.

"If it makes you feel better, I found another name you might be interested in."

In response to her confused look, he grinned.

"Percy Dawson. That is a man that, let's just say, I have some prior history with."

"I knew it!" Pen said before she could stop herself. Behind Jack, Tommy laughed silently.

"I'll be sure to send an *anonymous* tip to the boys in the NYPD. Consider that a bonus."

"I'd rather not?"

This time both Mr. Sweeney and Tommy laughed.

"I made it clear when I came to Tommy that I wouldn't do any of your dirty work for you, Mr. Sweeney."

"Come now, Miss Banks, after all we've been through together, you think I'd do you dirty like that? Especially now with all that money you have." He clucked his tongue and shook his head as though he was offended she had even suggested a thing. "No, you are far too valuable a...*friend* for me to use you that way."

"Why doesn't that fill me with relief?"

He grinned, that ruddy, boxing-scarred face of his showing not an ounce of humor. "I'll be in touch at some point, Miss Banks. When I do, I expect you to pick up the phone."

Pen frowned. She figured it would do no good to point out she was very close with a New York police detective. She knew Mr. Sweeney had far more connections with the NYPD than she did, most of it corrupt.

"Go on out there and have a drink on the house."

Penelope rose and exited the back room. She didn't take him up on the offer of a free drink; it would have tasted too sour. She caught Lulu's curious gaze and offered what she hoped was a reassuring smile. Her friend wasn't fooled, but didn't try and stop her as she left.

Pen could only wonder when this "friendship" of Mr. Sweeney's would be called upon.

EPILOGUE

By the time Sunday night came, Penelope had almost forgotten about her meeting with Mr. Sweeney. She certainly did her best to put it at the back of her mind.

Considering the company, it wasn't that difficult to do.

Richard sat across from her at the small table with a single candle offering soft lighting. Penelope had absolutely forbade them from going someplace that would be crowded with other couples celebrating the holiday, so they had meandered until they found a small, decidedly unromantic German restaurant.

Dot and Dash had gone to stay with Jacob Millington... for the time being. Their favorite dog walker had been hired by him, and Penelope suspected that same time next year, they might have a new home with her and her new husband, Dorothy Abernathy's nephew.

All the other men in Mrs. Abernathy's life were on their way to serving time for some crime or another. An anonymous tip had indeed come in about Percy Dawson's history of fraud, complete with proof. Beau hadn't done a very good job of hiding the stolen jewels, and he'd miraculously been discovered and arrested. Alan's assistant had eagerly squealed on him about his criminal activity and he wouldn't be seeing the outside of a prison for a long time, if ever. As for Mr. Comeau, Pen hoped Dot's bite was festering in the jail cell where he was currently sitting.

"So here's to our first official Valentine's Day," Richard said, lifting his ginger ale toward her. Pen breathed out a laugh and tapped her glass of the same to his.

"Prohibition really diminishes the romance," Pen sighed, wrinkling her nose after taking a sip.

"Is being with me so intolerable you need to drink?" Richard teased.

"You know that's not true."

"No, but you do have a point. I'd prefer to toast with a glass of red wine, or even champagne."

He leaned back and considered her. "Hopefully all our Valentine's Days won't be preceded by murder investigations."

"What fun would that be?"

He laughed, then studied her, his dark eyes glimmering in the single flame. "Should I move on to even more serious subjects?"

"Such as?" Pen asked innocently enough.

"You know what. Jane and Alfie have me thinking."

"And we agreed not to move too fast. It works for them. For us?" Pen tilted her head and smiled. "I only just discovered you had a dog as a pet when you were a child."

He nodded in concession. "That's fair."

"Besides," Penelope said, studying him more intently. "I have this odd feeling that we'll both just know when the time is right to get married."

He studied her just as intently, then breathed out a soft laugh. "Strangely enough, I have that same feeling."

Pen smiled and brought her head back up. "See? We're already on the same page. That said, you can *always* send me roses."

"Of course," he said with a grin.

"With baby's breath."

"Naturally."

"Not jewelry though."

"Good to know," he said grinning and lifting his glass in salute.

Pen laughed, then gave him a daring look. "And I suppose the occasional room at the Plaza wouldn't be out of order. After all, I've been informed these are modern times."

"*Extremely* good to know."

"Perhaps even...tonight?"

"I doubt they'd have a vacancy."

"True." Pen sighed heavily and looked idly off to the side. "I suppose I'll just have to settle for spending Valentine's night at your apartment?"

When she brought her gaze back to Richard he had a grin on his face. "I suppose you will, my dear."

AUTHOR'S NOTES

One of the things I love about writing historical mysteries is the wonderful little tidbits you come across. I knew I wanted to incorporate flowers into my story (because, Valentine's Day), so I did a bit of research in that regard.

FLOWERS

Mrs. Abernathy would have come of age in the Victorian era, when the language of flowers was a popular fad. With Dot and Dash playing a major role, I thought they deserved to have some part in the overall mystery, so I gave them their own bit of related peril. Rest assured, pets will never actually be murdered in any of my stories.

THE PANSY CRAZE

Benny's always-humorous yet ribald role in this story also came about after reading up on flowers. The Pansy Craze, as they called it was just one of the many aspects of the modern times we call the roaring twenties. Societal norms were changing in many ways and, while it wasn't entirely acceptable for men to publicly date men, it wasn't quite as scandalous as it had been even a decade prior. Still, many men kept things behind closed doors in private clubs.

The brief mention of the Hamilton Lodge for the Masquerade and Civic Ball was a fun tidbit I read about in an article online (For those of you reading print: https://queermusicheritage.com/nov2014hamilton.html). It was a wildly popular annual ball held in Harlem. The article claims that in late February 1926, nearly 1500 people attended, half of whom were men dressed as women. Oh, to be a fly on the wall...

GRAND CENTRAL SCHOOL OF ART

Yes, there really was a Grand Central School of Art located in Grand Central Terminal. It was founded by Sargent, Greacen, Clark, and others in 1922 on the seventh floor. There were several galleries also attached to it. It closed in 1944. Fiona Davis's *The Masterpiece* is a very enjoyable novel if you would like to know more.

VALENTINE'S FUN

I was in search of some fun Valentine's Day facts to sneak into this story and instead stumbled upon *Valentine's City of New York*. It was published in 1920 as both a guidebook and historical almanac of sorts. The most fascinating bit is that it boasts 160 full-page photos and 6 maps of New York. Talk about falling down the rabbit hole! If you enjoy the period that Penelope Banks is set in, and the history that led up to it, I highly recommend it. It's worth it for the photographs alone. You can find a digital copy freely available online here on archive.org (For those of you reading print: https://archive.org/details/valentinescityof00browa/page/n5/mode/2up).

GET YOUR FREE BOOK!

Mischief at the Peacock Club

**A bold theft at the infamous Peacock Club.
Can Penelope solve it to save her own neck?**

1924 New York
Penelope "Pen" Banks has spent the past two years making
ends meet by playing cards. It's another Saturday night at
the Peacock Club, one of her favorite haunts, and she has

her sights set on a big fish, who just happens to be the special guest of the infamous Jack Sweeney.

After inducing Rupert Cartland, into a game of cards, Pen thinks it just might be her lucky night. Unfortunately, before the night ends, Rupert has been robbed—his diamond cuff links, ruby pinky ring, gold watch, and wallet...all gone!

With the Peacock Club's reputation on the line, Mr. Sweeney, aided by the heavy hand of his chief underling Tommy Callahan, is holding everyone captive until the culprit is found.

For the promise of a nice payoff, not to mention escaping the club in one piece, Penelope Banks is willing to put her unique mind to work to find out just who stole the goods.

This is a prequel novella to the *Penelope Banks Murder Mysteries* series, taking place at The Peacock Club before Penelope Banks became a private investigator.

Access your book at the link below:
https://dl.bookfunnel.com/4sv9fir4h3

ALSO BY COLETTE CLARK

ABOUT THE AUTHOR

Colette Clark lives in New York and has always enjoyed learning more about the history of her amazing city. She decided to combine that curiosity and love of learning with her addiction to reading and watching mysteries. Her first series, **Penelope Banks Murder Mysteries** is the result of those passions. When she's not writing she can be found doing Sudoku puzzles, drawing, eating tacos, visiting museums dedicated to unusual/weird/wacky things, and, of course, reading mysteries by other great authors.

Join my Newsletter to receive news about New Releases and Sales!
https://dashboard.mailerlite.com/forms/148684/7267835648776731 8/share

Printed in Great Britain
by Amazon